Praise for *The Do*

If you have already met a young lady called Autumn, and her fluffy little dog, Chrissy, you'll look forward to following them with another murder investigation. If not, you are in for a pleasant surprise, and this story stands perfectly well alone.

I won't give any of the plot away, but here you'll find a light-hearted, often very funny, account of some serious events, and an even more serious love of dogs. The little town of Knollwood is the location of several murders. It helps that the principal investigator has the police detective in love with her.

Any book worth remembering has lessons under the surface. I approve of these ones. They are mostly about human nature, and the way good people treat each other. Read, and find out what I mean.

Bob Rich, PhD, author of *Ascending Spiral*

I have read several of Ms. Wing's books and as always she keeps me guessing till the end when all is revealed. I have fallen in love with Chrissy and Autumn and their continuing journey to health while finding themselves in the middle of a murder mystery adventure. My pre-teen daughter and I enjoyed reading *The Dog-Eared Diary* and then discussing the clues, plot twists and characters. I am looking forward to the next installment of Chrissy and Autumn's adventures!

Antoinette Brickhaus, Maryland

I love the world of *The Dog-Eared Diary* because we get many plot twists in a matter of pages. From thinking we have the culprit but then, plot twist, we are again searching for clues as to who the real criminal is. People of all ages will enjoy this book for sure as it is a one of a kind!

Veronica Brickhaus, Maryland

Loved this book! The second of the Chrissy the shih tzu mysteries tells the story of how a secret changes Autumn Clarke's life forever and how Autumn and Chrissy investigate the unexpected death of a prominent town member. We are reintroduced to Ray, Autumn's love interest, his ex-police dog, Ace, and several of Autumn and Chrissy's friends. A fun and engaging read! Looking forward to Book Three!!

Terri Chalmers, New Jersey

What a fun and captivating read! Diane delivers complex plot lines and a cast of memorable characters passionate about their canine companions and crime solving. A very original and satisfying story for mystery fans. I could not put it down until the very end.

An outstanding read! *The Dog-Eared Diary* is the second installment in Diane Wing's new series, but it stands alone as a solid page-turner. The two and four-legged characters we first met in Attorney-At-Paw are at it again, solving a decades-old missing persons case in a charming Pennsylvania town. A fresh, original storyline with rich historical overtones, surprising twists and turns, and characters you will be very sad to say goodbye to.

May there be many more adventures with Chrissy! This would make a GREAT television series! Someone, please call The Hallmark Channel!

Maxine Ashcraft, California

The Dog-Eared Diary

A Chrissy the Shih Tzu Mystery

Diane Wing

Modern History Press

Ann Arbor, MI

Library of Congress Cataloging-in-Publication Data

Names: Wing, Diane, 1959- author.
Title: The dog-eared diary : a Chrissy the Shih Tzu mystery / Diane Wing.

Description: 1st. | Ann Arbor, MI : Modern History Press, [2019] | Series: Chrissy the Shih Tzu mystery; #2 | Summary: "In this 2nd book of the mystery series, Autumn Clarke and her Shih Tzu dog "Chrissy" are compelled to solve a missing persons case that could be the result of foul play"-- Provided by publisher.
Identifiers: LCCN 2019030690 | ISBN 9781615994717 (paperback) | ISBN
   9781615994724 (hardcover) | ISBN 9781615994731 (kindle edition)
Subjects: LCSH: Missing persons--Investigation--Fiction. | GSAFD: Mystery
   fiction. | Suspense fiction.
Classification: LCC PS3623.I652 D64 2019 | DDC 813/.6--dc23
LC record available at https://lccn.loc.gov/2019030690

Published by
Modern History Press
5145 Pontiac Trail
Ann Arbor, MI

www.ModernHistoryPress.com
info@ModernHistoryPress.com
tollfree 888-761-6268
fax 734-663-6861

Distributed by Ingram Book Group (USA/CAN/AU), Bertram's Books (UK/EU)

This book is dedicated to my neighbors,

who are as dear to me as family.

Books by Diane Wing....

Cozy Mysteries with Chrissy the Shih Tzu

Attorney-at-Paw

The Dog-Eared Diary

Dark Fantasy

Coven: The Scrolls of the Four Winds

Thorne Manor and other bizarre tales

Trips to the Edge

Non-fiction

The True Nature of Tarot: Your Path to Personal Empowerment

The True Nature of Energy: Transforming Anxiety into Tranquility

The Happiness Perspective: Seeing Your Life Differently

Missing Person Report: Abigail Peabody, Knollwood, PA

Abigail Hempstead Peabody of Knollwood, PA was reported missing by her husband, Horatio Peabody, on August 7th, 1935. She is 5'6" weighing 115 pounds, with dark hair and brown eyes. She was last seen by her husband at the West Chester train station on her way to visit relatives in New York who said she never arrived. Anyone with information regarding the whereabouts of Mrs. Peabody should contact the Knollwood police department immediately.

Obituary: Horatio Peabody (1878-1957), Knollwood, PA

Wealthy local businessman, Horatio Peabody, died at home on July 13, 1957, after a short hospitalization, surrounded by his family. He is survived by his son, Maynard; daughter-in-law, Jillian Smith Peabody; and grandson, Edgar. He was a respected member of his community and donated 60 acres of land to Knollwood Township to be eternally preserved as a public park and recreation area. Services will be held at First Presbyterian Church of Knollwood at 93 Main Street, July 20, 1957.

≈ 1 ≈

The side of her fist slammed onto the polished desktop, moving the air toward Oxnard Peabody's face. He detached himself from her toxic energy by wondering why she never spent money on a manicure. Nail polish might ease her nail-biting habit and professional attention could smooth the jagged cuticles made by her relentless oral assault on her fingers.

"You're keeping something from me, and I want to know what it is!"

"The secrets I keep are for your own good, Beatrice." Oxnard sighed. His sister tested his patience on a regular basis. He never understood where her anger came from, always bubbling below the surface.

Beatrice folded her arms defiantly, her stance planted, unwilling to yield. Her expensive peach-colored cotton dress hung shapelessly on her lanky figure, with flat brown leather sandals cheapening the look. Oxnard took a deep breath, trying to reclaim the air Beatrice sucked from the room. Suggesting a stylist would send her through the roof. He had learned to divert his attention over the years to her appearance as a stress-management strategy when she was in attack mode.

They had been through all this before. Oxnard knew she was hell-bent on changing everything in her favor and discovering family secrets he promised his father he would keep. Oxnard dug his shiny black wingtips into the worn rug under his desk.

A sinister grin filled Beatrice's face. "I'm next in line to inherit the stone mansion."

"The house is not meant for you."

"Then for who?"

"Be happy with your trust fund and leave the rest to me."

"You don't even live there. Why not hand it over while you're still alive?"

"There is a reason I don't live there, Beatrice. Besides, Great-Grandfather Horatio left specific stipulations regarding the house."

Now that it's yours, you could change that condition."

His mouth turned down. "Don't you think I'd want to live in our family's legacy? And you along with me?"

"Aren't you afraid I'd kill you in your sleep?" she said with an unnerving smirk.

Even though his sister sounded as if she was teasing him, the thought had gone through his mind as a serious possibility. Oxnard had feared for his life many times after spats during their life under the same roof as children. Battles occurred for a variety of reasons: sibling rivalry, possessiveness over a toy or book, or academic envy, such as on days when their report cards reflected Oxnard's superiority. All triggered physical confrontations and consequential groundings. Oxnard was a quiet child, preferring books to people. From the day Beatrice appeared, his life had changed and his stress increased.

He struggled to hold his rolling executive chair in place the way he had held his fear around Beatrice. His deepest desire was to get far away from his sister's fury.

"I certainly hope not." Oxnard's voice was steady, but his pulse raced.

Beatrice let out a disbelieving growl. "What's the reason, then?"

"Father said the house was evil."

The look on Beatrice's face told him she was not buying the story.

"Oh, come on, Oxnard. You don't really believe that, do you? There's no such thing!"

Oxnard saw Beatrice's dark brown eyes flash the way they used to just before she sucker-punched him in childhood, and he knew that, in fact, evil did exist.

"He told me to protect you."

"I don't need protection, but you do." Beatrice grimaced.

Oxnard shook his head, suddenly exhausted.

"How many times are we going to have this conversation? Let it go."

"Not likely."

Oxnard let out the breath he did not know he was holding.

"Don't negate the family history. Think about how unlucky Great-Grandmother Abigail was in that house. She was ill before her disappearance. Great -Grandfather Horatio suffered from alcoholism. Grandfather Maynard lived there until Grandmother Jillian had a miscarriage. She refused to live there after that. Once they moved, they were able to have Father. Mother and Father chose not to live there to avoid the dread that surrounds that building and the bad luck that follows."

"I've heard the story before. You know as well as I do it was simple superstition and a series of unfortunate events that could have happened to any alcoholic and his family. The stress could have caused a miscarriage for our grandparents."

Oxnard sighed, as weary of the repetition as Beatrice. He had hoped the stories would compel her to believe the house was evil. He knew it was not. The only thing malevolent about the house was the heavy energy left by those who lived there. His family members were champions at creating negativity for each other, just as Beatrice did for him.

"I signed over Mother and Father's house to you and bought one for myself. Isn't that enough?"

Beatrice ignored his generosity and challenged Oxnard. "I could make the board of the Peabody Foundation decide." She shoved her glasses higher on her beaked nose with her middle finger.

"The Peabody Mansion is not part of the Foundation. It is mine. The board has no say in this matter. This discussion is over." Oxnard's innards felt like mush. He was ready for Beatrice to leave.

"I disagree. There's a way around everything, and I'm going to find it."

"Let's just get through the day, shall we?" Oxnard was tired by this discussion and by her presence.

A hard knock on the heavy wood-paneled door interrupted the argument. Oxnard was thankful to whoever was on the other side of the door. Beatrice pressed her lips together in frustration.

"Come in!"

Greg Manning, caretaker of Peabody Mansion and manager of the Peabody Festival, packed the doorway with his imposing muscular build and sandy blond hair. Greg had been a trusted member of the Peabody staff for the majority of his thirty-seven years, having started out of high school. Beatrice and Oxnard's father, Edgar, had hired him for a summer to care for the outside of the mansion. He had never left, and Greg's duties expanded.

His bold good looks and flirtatious ways made him a legend among the women in town. Oxnard had seen women practically swoon in his presence. At first, Oxnard could not understand why they fell for Greg's manipulations eighty percent of the time and competed for his attention.

Oxnard's own neat, book-smart appearance did nothing to win him a wife. Then again, his focus on work and family matters made him withdraw from social gatherings, which did not align with courtship. Charm was not his strong suit. He had reasoned that dependability is a trait women want, but discovered by watching Greg's amorous ways that flattery and attention worked better.

Beatrice glared at him. Oxnard noticed that Greg's wink and bright smile did nothing to melt the icy stare.

"Are you coming out soon? The place is getting mobbed and they're looking for the master of ceremonies to kick things off."

Oxnard did not enjoy public speaking and his argument with Beatrice did not put him in a social mood. This task would test his acting skills to the breaking point.

"Yes, as soon as we're finished with our conversation."

"I think we're done," said Beatrice, "for now."

Beatrice stormed out of the office and slammed the door behind her.

Greg stared after her and then looked at Oxnard, who shrugged. Greg nodded in understanding. He had experienced many fights between the siblings over the years. It was a way of life and a constant source of embarrassment for Oxnard.

"Give me a minute," said Oxnard.

"OK, boss," said Greg as he quietly closed the door behind him.

Oxnard stayed in his chair, praying that she would not ruin the annual Peabody Festival in honor of Great-Grandfather Horatio. A slight tremor moved through his body, as it did after each encounter with Beatrice. He wanted to love her, to take care of her, but she made that so very hard.

≈ 2 ≈

Autumn Clarke; her Shih tzu, Chrissy; and best friend, Stephanie Douglas, walked through the late-August heat shimmering over the annual Peabody Festival grounds. Packed with locals and visitors alike, the festival was an important part of Knollwood's economy. The town benefitted from the influx of tourists who patronized the bed and breakfasts, restaurants, and Main Street retailers. The number of vendors and booths at the festival seemed to double over last year, with rows of tents added to the center of the fair grounds and an expanded stage area.

Autumn and Stephanie scanned the schedule of speeches and bands. The map of vendor tables handed to them at the gate helped them strategize to visit as many booths as possible before twilight fell. Once it got dark, the blasts from the fireworks would upset Chrissy and make her whole body tremble. Autumn wanted to be home before that happened.

Autumn watched Chrissy's tail bounce up and down as her hips swayed side-to-side. Chrissy sniffed the freshly mowed grass and sneezed.

"Bless you, sweetheart," said Autumn.

Chrissy looked up at Autumn with a glistening nose, wagged her tail, and continued her joyful trot. Autumn watched her, proud that Chrissy had come such a long way in the four months since she'd lost her daddy and Autumn became her pet parent. Chrissy's resilience inspired Autumn to move past her own grief at the loss of her parents eight months before.

The soaring heat did not seem to bother Chrissy, despite her long, silky hair. The warm breeze cut into the humidity and blew through Chrissy's bangs. Autumn had the water bottle and portable cup at the ready in case her precious Shih tzu got thirsty

They strolled past lines of eager patrons waiting to cool down at the water ice, lemonade, and ice cream stands. They had started at the row to the right of the entry gate, and were about a quarter of the way through, stomachs growling as lunchtime approached. As if in response to their hunger pains, a bright yellow tent with bold flowing red font advertised Coleman's Kitchen. Autumn and Stephanie smiled at each other and sped-up the pace. Lisa Coleman greeted them with a big smile and open arms.

"Ladies! Thanks for stopping by!"

"We wouldn't miss it!" said Autumn and Stephanie in unison as if they planned it. The two women had been best friends since they roomed together at Villanova and often finished each other's sentences.

Stephanie's enthusiasm about Lisa's cooking skills began after tasting her crab quiche at Autumn's house. It was nice to have a neighbor so accomplished in the culinary arts.

Autumn was proud of Lisa's decision to pursue a career she loved, especially after the awful experience she had at the law firm she worked for this past spring. She had a couple of years left in her culinary program at The Restaurant School in Philadelphia, but that did not stop her from opening her own restaurant in the meantime. She'd learned to cook from her mother, who passed away from cancer, and found that she was a natural chef. Lisa's father, Steve Coleman, supported his daughter's dream. He and Lisa lived a few doors down from Autumn, and Steve was pet parent to Chrissy's best friend, Mickey the white standard poodle.

"How's business at the restaurant?" Autumn asked.

"Good. My biggest competition is Patsy's Deli, but my rotating menu keeps patrons tired of the same old lunch coming in. Patsy's makes breakfast, too, but I don't think I'll move into that. Maybe I'll start serving dinner or catering at some point, but with school, I just don't have the time to do anything but lunch."

They bit into the samples of Lisa's signature Mediterranean sandwich with lemon hummus, assorted veggies, and feta cheese on naan.

"Mmm," Autumn groaned, "this is so good."

Stephanie nodded, her mouth full.

Lisa beamed.

"Do you have a full-size version available?" Stephanie asked, looking around for a table. She spotted one at the corner of Lisa's tent.

"Yep. What do you want to drink?"

"Water's fine," said Autumn. "I'll take a Mediterranean sandwich, too, please."

Despite Lisa's insistence to the contrary, Autumn and Stephanie purchased their lunch. They were all for supporting their friend's enterprise. Lisa threw a couple of jumbo chocolate chip cookies on the tray as a bonus.

Enjoying the shade under the tent, Chrissy got her bowl of water and a grain-free snack and settled in the cool grass beneath the table. It was the perfect respite before continuing their exploration of the festival offerings. They perused the list of vendors and activities as they ate. A child ran by with his face painted like a tiger.

"I think we can skip the face-painting booth," said Stephanie with a chuckle.

"Agreed," said Autumn.

"Hi, Miss Douglas!" a little girl called from a nearby table.

Stephanie taught fifth grade at Knollwood Elementary school and often saw her students out and about.

"Hey, Cindy! Are you having fun?" Stephanie waved to Cindy's mother sitting next to the child. "Hi, Mrs. Tandy."

The woman waved, her mouth around a sandwich.

"You have Miss Jenkins for sixth grade, right?"

"Yeah," Cindy sounded disappointed.

"You're going to love her. She likes to have fun in her classroom. Plus, you're a terrific student, so you'll do great."

Cindy brightened and then spotted Chrissy. "Can I pet your dog?" Cindy asked with a sparkle in her eyes as she looked at Autumn.

"Sure, she loves the attention. Her name is Chrissy," Autumn said.

Cindy bent down and reached under the table. Chrissy came out, wagging her tail, to make it easy for the girl to reach her.

"Hi, Chrissy. You're so soft! Your bow is so pretty."

Chrissy's topknot set-off by a pink satin flower clip was a kid pleaser every time. Cindy's touch was very gentle.

"Hey! She just smiled at me!"

Autumn did not doubt it. Chrissy had an expressive face.

Stephanie saw Mrs. Tandy signaling for Cindy to return to the table.

"I think your mom wants you. I'll see you in a couple of weeks, OK?" said Stephanie.

Cindy nodded reluctantly, said goodbye to Chrissy, and went back to her lunch.

Brad Hall, another of Autumn's neighbors, walked by in his park ranger uniform, at the festival in an official capacity. He waved. Autumn knew his wife, Julie, was at the festival, too, operating the bake-sale booth to raise money for school activities.

"Let's go find Julie," suggested Autumn. She moved her finger along the festival map. "Her booth is a few down from this one."

They did not have to look hard, since Chrissy spotted her friend, Teddy the Yorkshire terrier before Autumn and Stephanie realized they had arrived at the booth. Julie and Brad were Teddy's pet parents. Chrissy pulled Autumn to where her friend stood, wagging his tail.

"Can I interest you in something to enjoy at home?" Julie smiled at them as she reached down to pet Chrissy. "How are you, little one?"

"I'm running low on snickerdoodles, so how about a small pack of those?" Stephanie dug in her purse for the money.

"I'll take a pack of chocolate chip cookies and that chocolate coconut Bundt cake."

Julie raised her eyebrows. "Buying for two, I take it?"

Autumn smiled. "As a matter of fact, yes. Ray has a sweet tooth."

"That's why he picked you, isn't it?" Julie laughed at her own joke. "You've gotten quite close over the last few months. You're the talk of the town."

"Well, investigating a murder is an intimate affair."

Autumn and Ray had solved the murder of Chrissy's original pet parent. Ray and his German Shepherd Dog, Ace, saved Autumn and Chrissy from getting killed themselves. "It's not every day you find a guy who is protective and understanding of my post-traumatic stress disorder."

Autumn had lived with PTSD for the eight months since the fatal car accident that killed her parents. She still missed them, but Ray brought his healing love to her rescue, as did Chrissy.

"One day I hope to find someone who loves me as much as Ray loves Autumn," Stephanie sighed.

"You will," Autumn said and squeezed Stephanie's arm.

Packages in hand, they said their goodbyes, after Autumn and Julie set plans to walk the fur babies together the following day. They stopped to play a few games, but did not win anything, laughing at each other's lack of accuracy at the ring toss and the shooting gallery. Halfway around the fairgrounds, they ran into Steve Coleman and Mickey. Chrissy's tail went into overdrive as she sniffed Mickey and hopped in greeting.

They walked past the hot dog stand, and Chrissy and Mickey's noses lifted to take in the aroma of the fragrant meat. Autumn's friend, Maureen Roberts, a local real estate agent, was taking her turn at the realty booth, surrounded by books filled with photos of available properties. The festival drew out-of-towners looking to relocate or purchase a second home.

Maureen had been friends with Autumn's mother and offered to sell Autumn's house when she was ready. Autumn was not sure she would ever be ready to leave the house where she grew up. It held too many memories, which both helped and hurt her progress in therapy. The constant reminder that her parents were gone was difficult, yet the familiar environment provided some solace. Then again, if things kept moving in the right direction with Ray, it could be time to get a place they could call their own. Stella and George Clarke had left everything to Autumn. She owned the house outright, but even if Ray moved in, it might always feel like *her* house rather than *their* house.

"I'm ready whenever you are, dear," said Maureen.

"You'll be the first one I call." Autumn smiled at the real estate agent's persistence. They had had this conversation a few times since Maureen found out about her relationship with Ray.

Autumn moved on with a friendly wave.

Screams came from the Round Up, a cylinder spinning so fast that riders were pinned to the wall. Autumn's group decided to stay on the ground. Feedback screeched from the loudspeakers, getting everyone's attention and forcing Chrissy to hide between Autumn's legs. Autumn lifted her up and hugged her close. Chrissy's paws sat on Autumn's shoulders, her furry head snuggled against her face. Autumn kissed her silky ear.

"It's okay," she whispered to Chrissy and then to her friends, "she'll be okay in a minute."

"Attention everyone! Our host, Oxnard Peabody, is about to take the stage."

Another screech of feedback exacerbated Chrissy's trembling. Her usually soft-smelling fur took on a mild pungent odor of fear. Autumn supported her head against her shoulder, bouncing her like a baby.

Autumn tried to distract her. "Look at Mickey! What's he doing?" but Chrissy only cuddled closer, so she resorted to making kissy sounds on her ear.

"Let's walk toward the stage. She'll calm down," Autumn said.

The group made their way across the grassy midway. Smells of popcorn, hot dogs, and cotton candy wafted on the air. The walking motion seemed to lull Chrissy, and the scented air caught her attention. Autumn felt her relax.

"Ready to walk?"

Chrissy lifted her head from Autumn's shoulder and made a grunting sound. Autumn placed Chrissy on the ground. She shook her luxurious white and charcoal gray coat and took her place beside

Mickey, who nuzzled her. Autumn, impressed by Chrissy's ability to regain her emotional balance, considered her a good example for her own recovery.

People stood behind the already-filled folding chairs. Greg Manning took the stage and tapped the microphone. Autumn checked on Chrissy, but the noise left her unfazed.

"Welcome to the eightieth Peabody Festival, celebrating the founder of this event, Horatio Peabody, and his generous donation of sixty acres of land to our community."

Greg waited for the applause to die down before continuing.

"Generations of Knollwood residents have enjoyed his legacy, and each year, our beautiful community draws thousands of visitors to Knollwood. We are glad to share this day with residents and visitors alike. Now, I'm honored to introduce Horatio's great-grandson, Oxnard Peabody."

The crowd applauded, with locals whistling and yelling Oxnard's name. The residents appreciated the Peabody family's generosity over the years and the festival was the most anticipated event for its fun and historical significance.

"Greg gets better looking each time I see him," said Stephanie.

"Have you ever met him?" Autumn asked.

"No, but I wouldn't mind. Let's see if we can bump into him before the day is over." A mischievous smile adorned Stephanie's lips as she clapped.

Oxnard waved his hands, encouraging quiet.

"Each year, the Peabody Festival expands to include more visitors and wonderful businesses. Great-Grandfather Horatio, would have been pleased to see how the celebration has grown and how much happiness his contribution to the community has brought to Knollwood. Thousands of feet have walked upon this ground to pay tribute to Horatio Peabody and his dedication to the community. We thank you for that."

The audience applauded and whistled, making Oxnard smile before raising his hands again to calm down the crowd.

"This year, there is a special surprise that very few people know about. I, Oxnard Peabody, am the featured victim at the dunking booth, wearing everything except my shoes. For the next several hours, you'll get to try your skill and see if you can soak me as I sacrifice myself for the cause. All proceeds from the dunking booth will go to the care and maintenance of Peabody Park and the Peabody Mansion Museum. We appreciate your support!"

Oxnard exited the stage to wild applause and laughter at the thought of this staid icon of the community being soaked, fully clothed, in the dunking tank. People started moving to get in line to try their hand at toppling him from his perch.

"I don't plan to participate in the dunking. There's no joy in seeing someone fall into water, plus I have lousy throwing skills," said Stephanie.

"I saw Greg walk over near the tent housing Jade's Jewelry. We can do a little shopping and see if you can get his attention."

Stephanie sucked in her cheeks and gave Autumn a big-eyed stare.

"What's the worst that can happen?" Autumn asked, and started walking toward the tent.

"I guess I could use some new jewelry."

"I have enough jewelry," said Steve, who tagged along with his dog.

Autumn chuckled. "You sure? How about some embellishment for Mickey?"

Steve smiled. "I'm heading to the hot dog stand. Mickey's been interested since we got here. I wouldn't mind one myself. We'll catch up with you."

Steve and Mickey headed toward the tantalizing smell of the hot dog vendor.

Autumn, Chrissy, and Stephanie made their way to the jewelry booth. Jade's had some of the best designer costume and natural stone jewelry and accessories in the area. The booth sparkled with necklaces, rings, earrings, beaded bags, and bracelets.

Jade Fisher, the shop owner, walked through the booth speaking with customers. She wore an extravagant labradorite pendant that practically filled the space created by the scoop neck of her peasant blouse. The iridescent sheen of the stone gave sophistication to her casual look. Her bleached-blonde hair puffed at the top and cascaded over her shoulders. Blue eyes peered out from lush black lashes.

Autumn watched Greg Manning walk to the corner of the tent and capture Jade's attention away from her customers with a wink and a smile. She beamed back at him and gave a slight nod. His broad shoulders and square jaw bewitched the unattached women in the vicinity, including Stephanie, who let out a little groan.

"Seriously? You're going to fall for that cheesy come-hither look? Besides, he's clearly selected his target."

Stephanie's raised brows dipped with realization. "Oh."

"Wait for the right one. Being alone is better than being with the wrong guy. Trust me."

"Yeah. I need some bling to get over it."

Autumn, Chrissy, and Stephanie systematically worked their way around the U-shaped table arrangement to make sure they did not miss anything.

They held up various pieces to judge the flattering quality and gave each other honest opinions. Autumn went for the earthier pieces, with opaque natural stones and fresh-water pearls attracting her attention. Stephanie liked flashier pieces; if it sparkled, it caught her eye.

Autumn spotted some rhinestone hairclips that looked perfect for Chrissy. The furry diva sat still while her mommy held up several designs for her. Autumn put four of them in her mini-shopping basket - two matching pink rhinestone clips for pigtails and one each of yellow and clear rhinestones for topknots.

"You'll look so pretty."

Chrissy looked at her and smiled.

"I don't see Greg," said Stephanie.

As they made their way to the back of the tent, Autumn heard some noises, but was not sure what they were or where they were coming from.

"Shhh, listen," said Autumn, her finger to her lips.

Now closer to the back of the tent, she heard two male voices, their tone angry but restrained, their growls muffled by the canvas curtains at the back of the tent.

"You can't be serious!"

"I've smelled it on you before and let it go, but being drunk at an important event is unacceptable. You're finished."

"But, I—"

Footsteps stomped away. Autumn looked down and saw Chrissy with her head halfway under the canvas looking at the commotion.

"Chrissy, come here sweetie."

The shih tzu pulled her head from under the curtain and sat next to Autumn, who crouched down beside her. Autumn whispered in Chrissy's ear.

"What did you see? Show Mommy."

A wave of nausea came over Autumn and a vision of wing-tip shoes walking away. The image faded.

"One of the men was Oxnard," she said to Stephanie.

"How do you know that?"

"I recognized the voice." Autumn felt bad lying to Stephanie. Even though Stephanie was her best friend and trustworthy, Chrissy's ability was an odd and unlikely gift that Autumn preferred not to discuss.

Maybe at some point in the future she would, but not yet. She was still coming to grips with it herself. Ray was the only other person who knew Chrissy's secret, out of necessity to solve the last case.

"What about the other one?"

"We saw Greg come this way, so it could have been him. I don't see him around."

Autumn heard the disappointment in Stephanie's voice.

"You may have just dodged a bullet. If he's an alcoholic, you don't want to date him no matter how handsome he is."

"True, but we still don't know if it was Greg. I'd rather give him the benefit of the doubt." Stephanie sighed and put a shimmering necklace in her basket.

They stepped over to the checkout area. Jade took each basket in turn.

"Find everything you wanted?" asked Jade.

"Probably more than I wanted," Autumn said.

"Do you have children? These rhinestone clips are perfect for fine hair." Jade put them in a little bag.

"Just this one," Autumn said, and pointed to Chrissy.

Jade bent down to pet her. "They'll look beautiful on her."

Chrissy wagged her tail.

Stephanie checked out without engaging in conversation.

They continued walking around the fairgrounds. Nearby, the sound of splashing and laughter rose above the din.

"Someone must have nailed the target and dunked Oxnard. Maybe it will cool him off."

"I hope so. I teach my students that holding onto anger hurts your heart."

A few booths down, Barbara McCarthy, owner of Attic Treasures Books, stood behind stacks of antiquarian and used books. Her short, wavy, dirty-blonde hair framed her gold-rimmed glasses, giving her a hip, librarian look. The ruffled, light-green sleeveless top brought out the tones of her hazel eyes.

Early on in their relationship, Autumn and Stephanie bonded over their love of books. They spent hours combing through library sales and used bookshops. Barbara had an extensive collection of out-of-print and hard-to-find volumes. She was also the town historian. The women knew Barbara from their frequent visits to her shop, as most locals did.

"Looking for anything in particular?" Barbara asked, giving a bright smile when she saw Chrissy.

"I'll know it when I see it," said Stephanie, already absorbed in the hunt.

"Me, too. We may be here for a while."

"Can this little girl have a snack?"

Chrissy was on a grain-free diet, including snacks, but Autumn did not like turning away kindhearted folks who wanted to give her a treat. Chrissy usually made the right decision to eat it or not.

"Sure."

Autumn watched Chrissy politely take the small bone-shaped cookie, hold it in her mouth while Barbara watched, and then place it on the ground as soon as she turned away.

Having found a few choice volumes in hardback, they headed across the field looking for Steve and Mickey. Autumn scanned the area. In the center of the open field, Chrissy stopped cold. Autumn gently tugged her leash to get her moving, but she would not budge. Chrissy barked until Autumn looked down, and then the dog began digging.

"What are you doing?" Autumn asked.

Chrissy's head stayed down, her claws rapidly displacing grass and dirt. No amount of encouragement coaxed her away from the spot. Several minutes later, Stephanie gasped. Out of the hole, a bony finger poked out of the ground, accusing an unknown perpetrator. Chrissy sat next to her discovery, panting through a layer of dirt speckling her white paws and underbelly. She seemed pleased to have unearthed the shallow grave.

Autumn whipped out her cell phone and dialed Ray. Stephanie went to find Brad Hall, the park ranger.

⚡ 3 ⚡

Brad stood guard over the finger until the police arrived twenty minutes later and officers taped off the area. A crowd clustered around the perimeter, vying for a glimpse as officers carefully dug around Chrissy's find and uncovered the rest of the skeleton. Tattered cloth hung from the bones.

A dripping Oxnard talked with Detective Ray Reed. Ray's German Shepherd Dog, Ace, guarded his flank. Autumn stood close enough to overhear the decision not to shut down the festival. People walked over the area for decades unaware that a body lay below the surface. With the discovery safely cordoned off, there was no reason to ask attendees to leave.

Autumn nudged Stephanie. "Look, there's Greg."

He leaned on top of the Whac-A-Mole arcade game, watching with a crinkled brow.

"If he's still here, then maybe he wasn't the one Oxnard was fighting with," said Stephanie, a note of hope in her voice.

"Maybe." Autumn was not convinced. They noticed Beatrice walk up to Greg. Their heads tilted toward one another in intimate conversation. Autumn wondered about their relationship.

Chrissy whimpered.

"I think your little excavator is hungry," said Steve. Mickey looked up at his daddy and licked his lips. "You, too, eh? Two hot dogs weren't enough?"

Mickey barked, catching Ray's attention. Autumn waved him over.

"Hey," Ray said, and then turned his attention to Chrissy. "Becoming quite the little detective, aren't you?"

Chrissy smiled and barked.

"Yeah, and you're getting a bath tonight," said Autumn.

Chrissy's ears went up as she recognized the word. No smile ensued.

"Ray, these guys are hungry. We're taking them home to eat dinner. Want us to bring Ace with us and feed him, too?"

"What do you think, buddy? Want to go to Chrissy's house?"

Ace wagged his tail. Now that Ace was a retired canine officer, he had the luxury of leaving the crime scene if a better offer came along. Ray handed Autumn the leash, his finger subtly stroking her hand. She knew he could not show overt affection while working, even though most of the town knew about their relationship. She liked the sensation of their private interaction.

"Thanks. Who knows how long we'll be here tonight. I ordered spotlights so we can keep working."

"We'll take good care of Ace until you pick him up, whatever time that turns out to be. Do you want us to bring back something for you and your team?"

"We'll be okay."

He nodded and waved to the group as he went back to the crime scene.

C380

They piled into Stephanie's deep blue four-door sedan. Autumn was glad Stephanie offered to drive. Even though the fatal accident was eight months ago, she was still skittish about oncoming traffic, which sometimes sent her into a full-blown panic attack depending on the size and proximity of the vehicle. Autumn straightened the blanket draped over the leather seat, tucked Chrissy snugly next to her, and clicked the seatbelt across them both. At least the blanket would get dirty rather than Stephanie's upholstery. Stephanie buckled Ace into the backseat, another blanket placed beneath him.

Steve and Mickey had their own vehicle, so they hung back to help Lisa pack up her booth. Deep twilight signaled the transition from marketplace to readying for the pyrotechnics display. Autumn watched the crowd in the vendor area thin out and move to the open field. Some had already spread their blankets and settled in for the fireworks.

"Where do you think Greg hangs out?" Stephanie asked as they pulled out of Peabody Park.

"What's on your mind?" Autumn had seen this behavior when they were in college. Every time Stephanie liked a guy, she would make herself look alluring and then make an appearance where her target hung out to see if he noticed her. If he did, then she would let nature take its course. If not, she would move on.

"I just want to see if there's a spark."

"Well, let's hope he doesn't hang out at the bar. Remember, Oxnard was angry because he smelled alcohol."

"But we don't know who that was."

"I don't know Greg's personal preferences."

Autumn stroked Chrissy and listened to her light snoring. Unlike Chrissy, Ace sat alert in the backseat with his head up, always on guard. They rode in silence for a couple of miles.

17

"Should we stop for food on the way to the house?" asked Stephanie.

"We could. How about a pizza?" Autumn dialed, and placed their order.

Stephanie swung into the parking lot of New Napoli and ran in to grab the food. A few minutes later, they pulled into Autumn's driveway.

☞ 4 ☜

Oxnard's queasy stomach could have been from the hot dog covered in sauerkraut or the slice of custard pie that followed. He skipped the fireworks for the first time in the festival's history, wanting to get home and out of his wet clothes. The hot shower did not help the shivering.

His hands prickled as he loaded logs into the fireplace in his study. The thought of building a fire in August seemed odd, yet he was willing to do anything to get warm. As the flames crackled the dry logs, Oxnard took his snifter of brandy and bundled up with his favorite fringed blanket.

He stared at the fire and sipped the golden liquid, feeling it warm the places the fireplace heat could not reach. His sister, Beatrice, popped into his mind, accompanied by thoughts of her incessant haranguing and the constant pushing for information she had no business knowing. The need to keep the darkest family secret from her weighed on him, but he took to heart the promise made to his father, Edgar. A shiver went through his body. He took another sip of brandy and adjusted the blanket.

Oxnard's life was one of stoic responsibility; he accepted the burden of being a public figure surrounded by difficult people. Had it finally caught up with him in the form of this sudden illness? He read somewhere that stress lowers the immune-system response. Could that be the explanation for the chills and flu-like symptoms?

The fire crackled and a spark jumped onto the stone hearth, its light quickly snuffed out before doing any damage to the nearby antique rug. That was Oxnard's life, his light barely a glimmer before his father saddled him with forbidden knowledge, followed by his own choice to withdraw, socially unencumbered to avoid the temptation to share his load. He played the role of figurehead, a sterile icon that brought no light to his community, a significant other, or himself.

It seemed a generational strain brought about by Great-Grandfather Horatio. Yes, Horatio bestowed money and other material gifts upon his offspring and to the town. Though posessing a spotless community reputation, within the family he was a mean drunk with little compassion for others. According to the oral family history, Horatio had displayed no remorse or concern at the disappearance of his wife,

Abigail. He reported her missing in 1935 and did all of the expected follow-up, but she was never heard from or seen again.

Oxnard took the last swallow of brandy and put the glass on the carved teak side table. His thoughts turned to the body found in Peabody Park. Horatio's legacy included something darker and more unexpected than his public persona. If that dog, Chrissy, had not dug up the skeleton, the secret might have stayed buried from the public eye. Now that it was exposed, he needed to get in touch with Autumn Clarke.

The fire was down to glowing embers, but Oxnard had no energy to rebuild the fire. He called his doctor instead.

⇶ 5 ⇷

Chrissy and Ace ran to the door barking before Autumn heard the key turn in the lock. Ray let himself in, greeted by a flurry of wagging tails and excited yips. Autumn watched him enthusiastically pet both of them, smiling, as happy to see them as they were to see him. Maybe his presence in the house did feel natural. It gave her hope that they could live here together one day.

It was 11:30 pm, somewhat earlier than she anticipated. She understood his long hours and was eager to hear about the skeleton after he had eaten.

Ray was trying to get past the welcoming committee and into the living room. Autumn laughed at the effort.

"Hey!"

"Hey, yourself. You must be starving."

"I am." Ray kissed her and went to the powder room to wash up.

Autumn went into the kitchen and from the oven pulled out a casserole dish filled with macaroni and cheese loaded with chunks of roasted chicken.

"That smells great!" said Ray. He settled at the kitchen table, with the pups sitting expectantly on either side of him.

"Let Daddy eat," Autumn told them and cringed. Was it too early to refer to him as Chrissy's daddy? "I have something better for you."

She got Ray's dinner on the table with a glass of water loaded with ice cubes the way he liked it, and then went to the treat cabinet. Chrissy and Ace followed her. She handed one treat to Chrissy, who took it gently. Ace's approach was naturally more aggressive, so she put the treats in his dish. He gobbled the chewy meat snacks in seconds. Chrissy held hers between her clean paws and nibbled at her snack. They looked at her for more.

"One more each, and that's it."

They ate those and went back to sit with Ray, allowing him to eat in peace. Autumn joined them with a cup of herbal tea, allowing Ray to fill up before starting a conversation. They often enjoyed comfortable silences. Their little family gathered in a quiet, loving circle wherever they were. Ray sat back, took a long drink of water, and smiled at her.

"Thanks, that was perfect."

"It gets better!"

Autumn gave him a choice between the chocolate chip cookies or the coconut Bundt cake she bought at the festival. Ray patted his stomach.

"Give me a few minutes, and then I'll have a cookie."

"Okay, let's go relax in the living room."

Autumn was getting used to Ray eating at all hours. Her habits were routine, but his random work hours dictated when he ate and slept. Ray nestled into his favorite spot on the couch, Ace on the floor at his feet. Autumn and Chrissy curled up next to him. She heard Ray let out a contented sigh.

"It doesn't get better than this," he said.

"Agreed. Want to watch TV?"

"No, I know you're eager to know what's going on."

"True, but I want you to wind down. You've had a long day."

He smiled at her and gave her a hug.

"I can do both. It helps to share it with you. Has Chrissy given you any clues about the skeleton?"

"No, she only showed me that Oxnard fired someone today for drinking on the job. That's got nothing to do with her discovery, though."

"He fired someone? Who was it?"

"I'm not sure. I didn't recognize the voice. I thought at first it was Greg Manning, but he was hanging around watching your team dig up the body, so it probably wasn't him."

"I spotted him, too. As the event manager for the Peabody Festival, that's not surprising that he wants to know what's going on. I need to question him tomorrow, along with Oxnard Peabody."

"Any idea who the skeleton belongs to?"

"The body seems to have been there a long time, and the tattered clothes appear to belong to a female. The style of the clothing might be from the early 20th century."

"Talk about a cold case! Mind if I dig around to get some historical information?"

"It couldn't hurt. My investigation is centering on living suspects for now. And my stomach is focusing on dessert."

"I'll bring you some herbal tea with your cookie."

Ray nodded and grabbed the television remote control.

⚞ 6 ⚞

The call from Oxnard Peabody's lawyer came early Monday morning. Autumn and Chrissy were just finishing their morning routine and ready to accommodate the strange request from the town celebrity. His house was five minutes away down lightly traveled back roads, so Autumn avoided the traffic that made her tense up.

Chrissy looked out the car window from her comfy car seat, fitted at the perfect height to enhance her view. She watched out for squirrels playing in the trees and on the lawns, barking when one ran into the road. Autumn was cautious of animals when driving, especially deer bounding across the street. Where there was one, there were likely others, including white-spotted fawns. When the deer sat in the backyard curled up beneath a tree, Chrissy sat spellbound, gazing at them through the sliding glass door.

They arrived at the large Queen Anne Victorian house sitting amidst expansive lawns and mature trees. The iron gates were open, allowing access to the property. Autumn pulled up in front of the wide front steps. She lifted Chrissy from her car seat and guided her to an inconspicuous spot to make sure she was empty before going inside.

The steps led to a wide front porch marked by white balustrades and tall French doors around the entire first floor. She banged the tarnished brass doorknocker. A man in a suit answered and waved them in.

"I'm Michael Thornburg, Mr. Peabody's attorney. Thank you for coming at such short notice."

"You're welcome. I'm a bit confused as to why he wants to see me."

"Mr. Peabody is very ill and needs to discuss an important matter with you. Right this way."

He led Autumn and Chrissy to the dark study where Oxnard Peabody lay bundled on the sofa before a blazing fire. The heat was overwhelming, especially coming from the muggy heat of outside. He looked pale, even in the firelight. It seemed like evening with the curtains drawn against the morning sun. Autumn positioned herself in Oxnard's view so he did not have to turn his head. The attorney gave him a sip of water and then sat in a chair opposite the couch. Chrissy sniffed Oxnard's fingers poking out from under the blanket. He touched her head.

"Hello, Mr. Peabody. I'm sorry you're not feeling well," said Autumn.

He barely nodded his head.

"The doctors don't know what's wrong with me," he managed. A wheeze followed, and then he said, "I must tell you something."

Autumn moved closer and sat on the floor next to his head so he did not have to strain to speak. Chrissy sat on her lap and looked at him. Autumn felt her concern. His hand shook and there was loose hair on his pillow. Patches of scalp showed through his dark hair. His pale skin had a yellowish tinge. She had not noticed that at the festival. He reached for Chrissy again and she leaned in so he could touch her head. It seemed to steady him.

Oxnard closed his eyes. Michael Thornburg sat silently, waiting for his employer to share his thoughts. The air in the room was heavy with heat and anticipation.

"The doctor is concerned that my time is short." Oxnard coughed. Autumn held the glass so he could sip water. "My Last Will and Testament was set in stone by Great-Grandfather Horatio. The Peabody Mansion and the majority of the family fortune are passed down according to Horatio's wishes — " He took a labored breath. "— along with the family secret." A coughing fit shook his body.

"Great-Grandfather Horatio passed control of the Peabody Foundation and millions of dollars in a trust to my Grandfather Maynard. He bequeathed the Peabody Mansion and the bulk of Horatio's estate to me."

"What does this have to do with me?" asked Autumn.

Oxnard pointed to the glass in Autumn's hand. She tilted the glass toward his lips.

"The rest of the estate, the Peabody Mansion and the majority of the wealth, goes to the last living Peabody — the grandchild of Allen Clarke."

"My grandfather? That doesn't make sense. What about Beatrice? Isn't she next in line?"

"No. She has a trust and my parents' house. She is not a true Peabody, but is unaware of that." Oxnard pushed past his labored breath. "My mother, Mary Jackson, adopted Beatrice from her cousin who was pregnant out of wedlock and had no one to support her."

"The adoption papers are sealed and the birth certificate amended to show the names of the adoptive parents."

Autumn put her hand on her head. Her heart went out to Beatrice.

"Trust us, Ms. Clarke. You have Peabody blood in your lineage. Beatrice does not. Horatio Peabody secretly fathered Allen Clarke with Daphne Clarke," said Michael Thornburg in a steady voice that belied the shocking news.

"How can you be sure?" Autumn's shock raised her voice an octave.

"Because Daphne's husband, Guthrie, was impotent," said Thornburg.

Autumn opened her mouth but no words came out. Chrissy panted, in rhythm with Autumn's short, shallow breaths.

"Guthrie Clarke accepted that Horatio was in love with Daphne. He went along and raised Allen as his own. You are the descendent of Daphne and Horatio."

Autumn looked at the attorney.

"It's true, Ms. Clarke," said Michael Thornburg. "We are hoping for Mr. Peabody's recovery, but in the event that he passes, the Peabody Mansion and the Peabody fortune are yours."

"Let's hope that doesn't happen, Oxnard!" She gently stroked his arm. "Why didn't anyone ever tell me this before? Did my parents know?"

Thornburg spoke for Oxnard as he labored to breathe. "Your grandfather, Allen Clarke, knew. His mother, your Great-Grandmother Daphne Clarke, swore him to secrecy until such time as it was necessary to share the information with his offspring."

"Did my dad know?" Autumn's eyes welled with tears thinking that her dad kept this hidden from her.

"We were obligated to inform him when Allen Clarke died. For public-relations purposes, he agreed not to tell you or your mother."

Autumn sat quietly, tears streaming down her face, aware only of Chrissy repositioning herself in her lap and the strained breathing of Oxnard Peabody. She looked up to find Oxnard looking at her.

"So we're related?" Autumn asked Peabody.

He nodded. "Second cousins."

Autumn thought for a moment. "So Grandpa Allen wasn't a blood-related Clarke at all, but rather an Adams-Peabody," she said. Great-Grandma Daphne's maiden name was Adams. That makes Dad and me Clarkes in name only!" She put her head in her hands. "I feel like my whole life is a lie."

Chrissy licked her arm and snuggled close. Autumn stroked her silky ears, which calmed her heartbeat.

"Does Beatrice know about me?"

Oxnard coughed. "No. She suspects something about the will, but does not know about the secret family history."

Thornburg jumped in. "She thinks that she is next in line to inherit the Peabody Mansion, as the last Peabody. She'll know that you are the true heir soon enough. One stipulation is that you are to keep Beatrice's true heritage to yourself."

"Be careful of Beatrice," Oxnard croaked. "She is an angry, bitter woman."

Thornburg rose to answer a knock at the door and returned with Doctor Anton Mortenson, Oxnard's physician. Autumn took Chrissy from her lap and moved away from the patient, plopping down in a chair. Chrissy found a spot on the floor next to her.

Doctor Mortenson acknowledged Autumn with a nod, and then turned his grim face to Oxnard Peabody's failing body. He took his pulse and his temperature, and listened to his heart. He folded his stethoscope.

"Oxnard, your eyes are yellow. Your liver is failing. We need to get you to the hospital right away." The already dense energy in the room thickened.

"No," Oxnard wheezed, "I hate hospitals."

"It's our only chance of saving your life!" Doctor Mortenson insisted.

"No."

"When did you start having symptoms?"

Oxnard was having difficulty speaking, so Autumn jumped in. "He was at the Peabody Festival. I saw him onstage speaking to the crowd. He looked completely healthy to me. And then he volunteered to be the target in the dunk tank to raise money for the Peabody Foundation."

The vitality Oxnard exhibited at the festival was gone, the life sucked from his body. He looked ancient for a man around sixty years old.

"I wasn't feeling well after that, so I came home. Missed the fireworks."

"Mr. Peabody, please listen to them and go to the hospital," Autumn begged.

He shook his head. "I'm tired of everything." He wheezed. "I'm tired of the secrets—the lies." He gasped for breath. "Tired of the responsibility — so tired."

"Does he live here alone?" Autumn asked the attorney.

"He has a house manager, Jasper Wiggins, but I haven't seen him."

Oxnard growled the word *fired*.

"You fired him?" asked Autumn.

Oxnard nodded.

A tear dripped down Autumn's face. How sad that he was so alone. Tired of carrying the family secrets, Oxnard was ready to die even though there was a chance for healing instead. Oxnard could rest easy now that he effectively transferred his burden onto Autumn's shoulders. The weight of it gave her a taste of what Oxnard had been living with all of these years.

She looked at the doctor and the lawyer in turn.

"Is there anything I can do for him?"

"Not unless you can convince him to get treatment," said the doctor.

"Is there anyone coming to care for him? Maybe Beatrice?"

"If she shows up, it would be as a vulture to pick the meat off his bones," said Michael Thornburg, his mouth twisting as though eating a lemon.

"Chrissy and I will stay with him."

Chrissy looked up at Autumn and whimpered. Autumn kissed her head.

"That's very kind of you, Ms. Clarke. I'll schedule a nurse to come as soon as possible to take over," said Doctor Mortenson. "In the meantime, here are a list of instructions and my cell phone number."

Hearing the doctor call her Ms. Clarke made her feel disconnected from the name she identified with all of her life, now knowing she was really a Peabody.

"Please come to my office in the morning to sign paperwork," said the lawyer. He handed her a business card with the address and phone number.

"I will."

The men left; the sound of the front door closing behind them made the house feel as empty as her heart. She saw her newfound cousin shivering under the thin blanket and fetched a thicker one from the ottoman. She gently tucked it around him.

"Thank you. I'm sorry we didn't— get to know each other— under better circumstances," Oxnard wheezed.

"Me, too."

Chrissy jumped up onto the couch and settled next to Oxnard. Autumn saw the worry in her eyes. He smiled and closed his eyes.

≈ 7 ≈

Autumn and Chrissy were relieved of their duty when the homecare nurse arrived around two that afternoon. The nurse was not happy that Oxnard was on the couch rather than in bed, and had a dog lying next to him. Autumn convinced her that he wanted Chrissy with him and that it would be torture to move him upstairs. She reluctantly agreed.

Autumn moved Chrissy so that the nurse could run through her checklist, Autumn and stayed another hour to make sure the nurse had the temperament to care for someone so ill. Chrissy watched intently. Autumn trusted Chrissy's excellent judge of character and was glad when she sent waves of approval to Autumn. Still, Autumn was reluctant to leave, worrying that this was the last she would see of Oxnard. He grew weaker before her eyes. What was left of his hair and scalp were wet with sweat from the heat he barely felt.

Autumn whispered one last plea to go to the hospital, but he grimaced in response. There was nothing more she could do. She touched his cheek and told him she and Chrissy would be back later. He blinked his eyes. A tear rolled down the side of his face. Autumn touched his trembling arm through the blanket.

The nurse gave him a shot of painkiller and then ushered them out, assuring them that she had things well in hand. *That may be*, Autumn thought, *but this could be the last time we see him alive*. The second thought was of Beatrice. *Where was she?* The man Beatrice assumed was her brother, her only remaining family member, was on his deathbed, and there was no call or knock at the door. Autumn hoped that the attorney was wrong about Beatrice being a vulture. She wondered if anyone had notified her or even Greg Manning, for that matter. He had known Oxnard for years. They had a relationship, and Autumn was puzzled at his absence.

Being that she was the long-held family secret, she did not want to contact either of them. When she got home, her first call was to Ray, leaving a brief message to call her, and the second call was to Michael Thornburg.

"Law office," answered the receptionist.

"May I please speak with Michael Thornburg? This is Autumn Clarke."

"One moment."

"Ms. Clarke, how can I help you?

"I just left Oxnard in the care of a nurse. He seems to be getting worse. Has anyone called his sister?"

"I believe Dr. Mortenson called Beatrice."

"Hmm."

"Are you able to come to the office tomorrow morning? Say around ten?"

"That should be fine. I'll see you then."

Autumn hung up, wondering why Beatrice had not come to the house. Autumn's concern for Oxnard as an ill, lonely person and newfound relative seemed greater than his own sister's.

Autumn gave Beatrice the benefit of the doubt; maybe the doctor was not able to get a hold of her. Autumn hoped to have a relationship with her, despite Oxnard's warning that she was an angry and bitter woman. It was possible that their relationship could be different, and Autumn wondered if Beatrice liked dogs.

Chrissy sat at the sliding door, patiently waiting for Autumn to notice her.

"You want to go out, sweetheart?"

Autumn opened the door, and Chrissy trotted across the patio and over to her favorite spot in the grass. Autumn watched her, making sure no hawks, foxes, or kidnappers disturbed her. Ever since a kidnapper had grabbed Chrissy a few months ago, Autumn became more vigilant than ever. Chrissy trotted back to the cool air of the house. This summer had been hot and muggy, and they both looked forward to cooler weather in the next couple of months. Chrissy walked over to her crystal water bowl and took a long drink, then joined Autumn on the sofa.

The laptop was open on the coffee table. Autumn searched for entries about the Peabody family, the Peabody Mansion, and each family member. Oxnard's admission that he fired his house manager was something for Ray to follow up on.

The house manager disappeared after the firing. The same day, Oxnard was fine one minute and on his deathbed the next. Was this a case of revenge for the firing?

The Internet search produced hundreds of stories about the family, their generosity to the community, and the disappearance of Abigail, Horatio's wife. There was nothing about Daphne or any illegitimate children. Having Daphne as a mistress and mother to his son was a good motive for murdering his wife. Was there a way to determine if the skeleton in the park was Abigail Peabody?

Chrissy pulled Autumn from her thoughts with a *grrr*. A flash of Oxnard lying limp on the couch came to mind. She dialed the nurse's cell number and discovered that Oxnard was no longer of this world. He passed shortly after Autumn and Chrissy left. Only the nurse was there at his transition.

Autumn cried for his lonely end, not even his sister there to give him comfort. Chrissy's big brown eyes glistened with sorrow. Autumn hugged her close, as they shared their sadness for Oxnard and wished his spirit the joy in the next world that he missed in this one.

⚜

Autumn was still in a stupor when Ray and Ace came over. Chrissy had not barked when they turned the key in the door. Ace went nose-to-nose with Chrissy. Autumn looked up at Ray, feeling the puffiness of her eyes. He stroked her hair.

"Babe, what's wrong?"

"Oxnard is dead."

Ray dialed a number and walked into the entry foyer speaking in low tones. Autumn watched him walk back into the living room.

"I just ordered the body to be transported to the medical examiner's office."

Autumn nodded. She silently agreed that Oxnard had been healthy one minute and critically ill the next.

"Have you eaten? How about Chrissy?"

That was when Autumn realized it was almost nine in the evening. Neither of them had eaten anything. She shook her head.

Ray went into the kitchen. Autumn heard him call for Chrissy and Ace. Chrissy looked at Autumn to get the go-ahead before leaping from the couch. She heard the furry friends lapping water and eating their meal. Ray emerged with iced tea and egg salad sandwiches, putting hers on the coffee table in front of her. She gave him a weak smile.

Ray sat next to her and hugged her close.

"I know how compassionate you are, but why are you so upset? You hardly knew Oxnard Peabody."

"He's my cousin."

Ray's mouth dropped. They ate as she told him almost the whole story, holding back the part about Beatrice being adopted.

"Since Beatrice didn't know about the stipulations in the will, she may have had motive to kill Oxnard to get her inheritance."

30

"I guess that's a possibility. But she gets a healthy trust and his house."

"Still, you better be careful. Once she finds out that you inherited from her family, she may plan to do the same to you."

The thought of that possibility made a chill run the length of Autumn's body.

"In the meantime, I'll see who else may be involved in Oxnard's death."

"It could be the person he fired." Autumn found herself protective of her cousin Beatrice. "Oxnard said he fired his house manager, Jasper Wiggins. He wasn't there when I was at the house."

Chrissy and Ace came running in from the kitchen, faces moist from dinner.

"Want to go out?" Ray got up and opened the sliding glass door to the backyard.

"Please watch her."

"Ace is with her. He'll guard her with his life."

Autumn smiled. "You're right."

Ray sat next to her and held her tight. He kissed her lips. "Just like I'll guard yours."

⇒ 8 ⇐

Autumn and Chrissy walked into Michael Thornburg's law office. She had no idea what to expect. Once Autumn was seated on a burgundy leather chair in Thornburg's formal but comfortable office, he pulled out a thick file.

Opening it, he said, "The Peabody file has been with this office since Horatio first came to see my great-grandfather to set-up the will. Horatio Peabody created a generation-skipping trust when he discovered that Daphne Clarke was pregnant. He made sure to take care of his great-grandchildren born of both his sons, Allen Clarke and Maynard Peabody. When Abigail Peabody disappeared, the townspeople suspected murder, but nothing was proven. Horatio's generosity to the community silenced those who tried pressing the issue with the local police."

Michael Thornburg folded his hands over the file. Autumn waited.

"When he inherited, Oxnard took part of the fortune and created a generous trust for Beatrice. He added her to the Peabody Foundation Board of Directors. She never knew that Oxnard ensured her wealth and status.

"The trust has a no-contest clause in it that stipulates that if Beatrice goes to court over the benefits provided for you, she stands to lose everything. Oxnard left Beatrice his personal house. The Peabody Mansion and the bulk of the estate go to you, Autumn."

Autumn frowned.

"I know this is a lot to take in, and the legalities of the will and trusts are complex, but the bottom line is that you are the sole benefactor of the Peabody fortune. No probate is required, as your name appears on all pertinent accounts and real estate. This means that you have access to your inheritance immediately."

She took a deep breath and picked up Chrissy, holding her close.

"I'm trying to adjust to the family history and to people suspecting Horatio of murdering his wife. To think that my great-grandmother had an affair that might have resulted in murder is upsetting enough, let alone what Beatrice is going to think about all of this."

"Don't worry about Beatrice. If she contests, I'll take care of representing the Peabody Estate on your behalf. If she tries to contact you, refer her directly to me. It's best not to engage with her; no good will come of it."

Autumn wrung her hands. Chrissy shifted in her lap. Autumn's hand stroked Chrissy's side, lessening her anxiety.

"Here are the keys to the mansion."

In taking the heavy silver keychain, the transfer of power was complete. Autumn squeezed it, saying a silent prayer for Oxnard to find peace.

"One more thing, Mr. Thornburg. Have you heard from Oxnard's house manager?"

"No one has heard from Jasper Wiggins since the festival."

"Will you let me know if he turns up?"

"Of course."

Autumn stood and shook his hand. Her mind whirled with the lies and deception her family had lived with for generations. She suspected that there was more to this story, and she was determined to find out the whole truth.

☙❧

Chrissy paused in the grassy area outside the attorney's office while Autumn dialed Stephanie.

"Hey, Autumn."

"Hi, Steph."

"What's going on? You don't sound quite yourself."

"I just left the attorney's office and feel a bit shaken up. Can you meet me at Coleman's Kitchen? I'm heading there now."

"Be there in a jiff!"

Autumn and Chrissy took a seat outdoors under an awning. A breeze tempered the heat. With five other customers inside the restaurant, Autumn wanted privacy when she shared the news with Stephanie.

They watched Stephanie pull up. The necklace she bought at the Peabody Festival glittered in the sunlight. Autumn admired Stephanie's style. The jewelry made a statement with her stretch jeans and white T-shirt. Chrissy grunted as Stephanie approached and looked up at Autumn, making sure she saw their friend.

"I know, Sweet Pea. Good girl." She reached down and stroked Chrissy's head, the soft hair soothing Autumn's nerves.

Stephanie stepped onto the patio. She acknowledged Chrissy and hugged Autumn. Lisa came out and joined them.

"Hi, Stephanie. Not many days left before school starts, eh?" said Lisa.

"I've already started gathering decorations for my room. I put finishing touches on my lesson plans last night."

"Lucky kids," said Lisa.

Autumn nodded her agreement.

"Let me guess; unsweetened iced tea for you both and a bowl of cool water for the munchkin?"

"And two of those Mediterranean sandwiches you served at the festival. I think I'm addicted to the lemon hummus," Stephanie said.

"Coming up!"

Autumn appreciated Stephanie dealing with the mundane act of ordering. Her mind, split between Oxnard's deathbed and the attorney's office, was overwhelmed. Stephanie put her hand on Autumn's.

"What's going on in that head of yours?"

Autumn looked up, feeling tears welling. She took a deep breath and dabbed at the corners of her eyes with a napkin.

"Oxnard died yesterday."

Stephanie sat back. "What happened?"

"His body started failing him after the festival. Chrissy and I were with him towards the end. She was such a comfort to him. Only a nurse was there to witness his last breath. No friends. No family. We shouldn't have left him."

"How sad. What were you doing at his house? You barely knew him."

"I was summoned by his attorney. Apparently, I'm related to him."

"Excuse me?"

Autumn told her the story of her family minus Beatrice's adoption. Stephanie's mouth was open almost the entire time.

"The bottom line is that I'm heir to the Peabody estate, including the Peabody Mansion."

"No way! Are you kidding me?"

"Nope." Autumn dangled the key with a solid silver *P* on the keychain.

"It's so strange. Oxnard seemed fine at the festival."

"Agreed. The medical examiner is doing some tests on the body. He refused to go to the hospital. I think they could have saved him."

"That's sadder still. How do you feel about all of this?"

"My life is a lie."

"It's exciting to know you're part of a local legend."

"Maybe, but everything I thought I knew about my family is—What I considered to be my heritage is—" Autumn sighed finding it difficult to pin down the sentiment.

"You're still the same Autumn I've always known and loved, except wealthier." Stephanie smiled.

Autumn sipped her tea and cleared her throat.

"I guess. It's a shame that all these years my dad kept it from me. In the eight months since my parents passed away, I felt so alone, but had relatives I could have gotten to know. Oxnard seemed like a nice guy — troubled, but a decent person."

"You still have Beatrice."

"I don't know about that. Oxnard warned me away from her. So did his attorney."

"I find that it's better to judge a person on your own rather than based on someone else's experience. Maybe she'll be different with you."

"We'll see."

"By the way, you're never alone. You have Ray, your neighbors, Chrissy, and me."

"I know. All of you guys are my family."

"Always and forever."

Stephanie squeezed her hand.

"I've never been to the Peabody Mansion, have you?" asked Autumn.

"Once when I was a child my parents took me to the Peabody Museum. I think it's part of the mansion itself."

"Feel like taking a ride over there after we eat?"

"Definitely! I want to see your new house."

"I don't know what I'm doing with it yet."

"Have you talked it over with Ray?"

"Not yet. I'm still in shock from the news."

"Let's see how you feel once you walk into the lap of luxury." Stephanie smiled and took a sip of her iced tea.

CΘ૪Ο

Stephanie had an idea where they were going. Autumn buckled herself and Chrissy into the passenger side. The air conditioning blasted in their faces.

They were in a part of the neighborhood Autumn had not played in as a child. It was just under two miles farther from her house, in the opposite direction of their usual walking route. A road sign up ahead indicated a no-outlet street called Evergreen Road, aptly named for the massive eastern hemlocks that stood guard over the roadway. Another sign pointed to the Peabody Museum parking area.

35

Stephanie made a left onto Evergreen Road. Only four houses were on the street, with about an acre between them, each one unique. They drove past a cottage-looking house with a charming addition that included large windows to bring in the outdoors. Most of the other homes had stone accents. They drove to the last house on the right-hand side. The street ended in dense woods that also surrounded the mansion and went as far back as the eye could see.

"I wonder if these houses were built on land that used to be part of the Peabody Mansion," said Stephanie.

"Maybe the township office has old plot plans," Autumn said.

Autumn took note of the house number 1111 as they pulled into the end of the long driveway. She had researched for an article on the spiritual meaning of numbers, and eleven-eleven symbolized synchronicity and new beginnings.

As they idled down the driveway, the building came into view through the trees. Autumn gasped. They stared at the massive, gray-stone Tudor Revival, surrounded by American beech trees to compete with the hemlocks. It dwarfed the other houses on the street. Dappled sunlight shimmered across the bluish-gray slate roof, leaded glass windows, and turrets and over the arched front door painted in oxblood red.

In childhood, Autumn had dreamed of living in an enchanting stone house in the woods. She never thought it existed in reality, yet here it was. Chrissy looked up and wagged her tail.

"I like it, too, sweetheart."

"Wow. You can't even see the end of the mansion for all the trees," Stephanie chimed in.

They pulled into the large parking lot at the back of the property.

"This is the museum parking lot. We have to find where the private residence parking is, but this will do for now," said Stephanie.

"I wonder how the residents of this street like all the traffic from the museum."

"I don't imagine there is that much traffic year round. Maybe around tourist season, but that's probably the only time. The real question is, how will you feel about the traffic when this is your home?"

"Again, I haven't made that decision yet," said Autumn and smirked at her friend.

They got out of the car. With steps as quiet as their surroundings, they moved past the shrubs and tall tree trunks, the temperature several degrees cooler under the trees. The sound of a stream rushing over rocks broke the silence.

Chrissy pulled on her leash, eager to explore her new surroundings. She sniffed along the ground as they moved past the museum entrance and through a small gate to a private slate walkway. Autumn felt as though she was intruding until she reminded herself that this was her house now. Chrissy marked a spot and continued to lead the way.

The stone path took them to the end of the structure and bent to the left. They followed it halfway down the building before Chrissy growled and then let out a slow, deep series of barks.

"What is it, Chrissy?"

"Probably nothing," said Stephanie.

"Yeah, that's what I used to think, but she knows when something or someone is nearby."

A moment later, Greg Manning stepped around the corner, blocking their way. He looked much bigger up close than he had from a distance when they saw him at the carnival. Chrissy's bark became more urgent. She stood in front of Autumn as though she were a fierce wolf defending her territory.

"What are you doing here? This is private property. I'm the caretaker, Greg Manning," he said.

"Yes, it is. Since it's now my property, I guess you work for me." Autumn folded her arms through the leash. Chrissy continued growling.

"I work for Oxnard Peabody. This property belongs to him."

"Not anymore. Upon his death, this property transferred to me."

Greg Manning took a subtle step back. "What?"

"That's right."

"Why wasn't I notified?" Greg's indignant tone implied he had more rights to information than a mere caretaker.

"Mr. Thornburg, the attorney, is in charge of the details. Feel free to call him with any questions."

"What's his number?" Greg asked as he retrieved his cell phone from his pocket.

Autumn recited the number. The secretary put Greg through to Michael Thornburg. Greg demanded to know what was going on and received confirmation that Autumn was, indeed, the new owner. His face soured, and he hung up.

Autumn held out her hand. "I'm Autumn Clarke." The name rang hollow with the new knowledge of her heritage.

"And I'm Stephanie Douglas." She giggled as she held out her hand. Greg ignored her. Stephanie's hand fell to her side.

"Does Beatrice know?" Greg grumbled.

"I'm not sure. I'd be grateful if you'd let us get on our way."

Greg Manning hesitated before stepping aside. "I can show you the way to the private residence. Do you have a key?"

"Yes, do you?"

"I do. I'm the caretaker of this property. I have access to all areas."

Autumn decided to review his access and then change the locks.

"Lead the way," Autumn instructed.

He turned and started down the path. Chrissy stopped growling and followed him with Autumn and Stephanie bringing up the rear. Autumn turned back to make sure Stephanie was behind her and caught her waggling her eyebrows and smiling. Autumn shook her head no; Stephanie responded by nodding yes. Autumn faced forward, giving up the silent fight.

"How many acres is the property?" asked Autumn.

"Thirty acres of land spread out that way," Without turning to address them, Greg pointed toward the deep woods that hid any houses that might be nearby.

The slate path curved again, and they came out to what looked like the front of the building. Autumn had a hard time thinking of this as a house or a home. The immensity made it seem like a school or other commercial enterprise. The stone pattern surrounding the arched doorway, with smooth rectangular stones pointing outward, was different from the horizontal stones that made up the majority of the structure. The design made the entrance feel important and regal, emphasized by the heavy wood door with dark, hammered metalwork hinges, knocker, and knob.

"Where is the private driveway to get to this entrance?" asked Stephanie.

Greg Manning pointed through the trees to the left of the entrance. "See the paving over there? That's the driveway. You have to go past the museum parking to the end of the building and turn in."

"Noted," Stephanie said, feeling like his answer opened the way for a potential conversation.

Greg Manning dug in his pocket for the key. It slid smoothly into the lock despite the years of abandonment the house had suffered. He pushed the door open. It glided quietly on its hinges. He entered first and flipped light switches as he went deeper into the foyer. Antique sconces with flame-shaped bulbs dimly lit the cavernous entry hall and the staircase winding along the wall accented by a wrought iron railing.

Chrissy went next, assessing her surroundings. Her big brown eyes took in the new environment. Autumn watched her reaction, trusting Chrissy to notice any lingering untoward energy.

Autumn and Stephanie gaped at the stone walls, small leaded glass windows near the top of the fifteen-foot ceilings, and giant walnut reception table with an empty vase in the middle standing on the gray slate floor. It was like stepping back in time. Autumn imagined her great-grandfather walking the halls and managing the business of a twenty thousand square-foot house. She reminded herself that the original living quarters included the attached museum.

"Why didn't Oxnard or Beatrice live in this house?" asked Autumn.

"Oxnard swore it was cursed since family members who did live here suffered from alcoholism, depression, and miscarriage to name a few. It's been empty for at least twenty years," said Greg.

Despite the August heat, Autumn felt chilled in the large space. She assumed that the stone walls and shade trees were likely the reason. If she did choose to live here, her air conditioning bills would be low. There was a mild smell of mustiness, but other than that, Greg seemingly kept the house well maintained.

Autumn removed Chrissy's harness so she could explore on her own. She went in the opposite direction, nose to the ground. The rest of them went through archway after archway, into the immense living room punctuated by huge arched windows allowing a view of the forest and a cushioned window seat. Autumn suspected that if she did move into this house, this would be her favorite spot. They walked into a surprisingly modest kitchen with an old-fashioned stove, freestanding wood cabinetry, and a thick porcelain sink. They went up the back staircase to check out the second level.

The bedrooms were spacious with windows of various sizes, all looking out upon the woods that surrounded the house. The master bedroom closets were shallow, making the renovation list for installing proper closets. The plaster walls had some minor cracks in them that should be easy enough to repair. Autumn's father had taught her how to spackle the walls of their home. Too bad George Clarke-Peabody was not here to help her now. He would relish the challenge. Besides, this house was his legacy, too. It was odd thinking of her father's name hyphenated to reflect the truth.

Autumn wondered if Ray would like sleeping in this room, and then shook away the thought, reminding herself that even though it felt much longer, they had only been together for four months. That was too soon to contemplate a lifetime together.

Ten bedrooms and six bathrooms were upstairs, and one bathroom downstairs. Of the twenty total rooms, the library was one of her favorites. The shelving, all loaded with books, covered every wall. The house was completely furnished. What made the family leave everything behind? Was the curse for real?

With Autumn lost in thought, Stephanie tried chatting up Greg, who paid little attention. Autumn could hear her talking but not the words she was saying.

Descending the main staircase, Autumn saw Chrissy gallop out of the den. Autumn bent down and lifted Chrissy into her arms. Chrissy grunted and made little mewling sounds into Autumn's ear.

"What did you see, baby?" whispered Autumn. She put her head against Chrissy's soft forehead.

A wave of mild nausea was followed by a vision of a tattered leather journal embossed with a rose. It peeked out from under the skirt of an upholstered chair in the den. The vision faded, and Autumn kissed Chrissy's head. She kept the vision to herself, wanting Greg Manning to leave before she retrieved the journal.

"Have we seen everything?" Autumn asked Greg.

"Pretty much, except for the basement and the attic. Both run the full length and width of the house. It's kind of dusty in the attic and the basement is dirty, so I don't recommend going down there unless you're wearing work clothes."

Greg showed Autumn the door to the basement, which was tucked in an alcove off the main foyer.

"The attic door is off the upstairs hallway."

"Thank you for the tour," said Autumn.

"Yeah, thanks," Stephanie said, batting her eyelashes at Greg.

Autumn rolled her eyes.

"We can take it from here."

"What will happen to my job?"

"Let's sit down and go over your duties at another time. I'll call you to arrange a meeting."

They exchanged cell phone numbers.

Autumn felt strangely aristocratic having to meet with a staff member who may or may not be employed by the end of the week. She could afford it, but that was not the issue. She was not sure she trusted Greg Manning. She wanted Ray there to manage any reaction from Greg and to question him about his possible involvement in Oxnard's death.

As Greg turned to leave, Stephanie blurted, "Hope to see you again soon."

He looked at her, nodded, and left, leaving them alone in the foyer.

"What do you think?" asked Stephanie.

"The house is bigger than I expected."

"That's not what I mean!" Stephanie tilted her head toward the door implying Greg Manning.

"I think that you're a shameless flirt, and he wasn't buying it."

"I'll grow on him."

"We don't know him that well. Reign it in a bit for now just to be safe."

Stephanie smiled. "Let's see what happens."

Autumn walked toward the den. "I want to check out this room. Chrissy saw it, but we didn't."

It was a comfortable space with walnut paneling and upholstered furniture. She looked for the chair Chrissy showed her and saw it at the far end of the room. Poking out from behind the chair was the leather cover of a book. Several ribbons bookmarked various places within it. Chrissy stood nearby wagging her tail.

"Good girl," said Autumn and petted her head, noticing her bangs needed a trim.

"What's that?"

Autumn opened the book. "Looks like a diary. It's handwritten."

"Does it say whose diary it is?"

Autumn flipped to the first inside page. It read, "This book belongs to Abigail Peabody – started on August 13, 1915."

"Do you think it's worth anything?"

"I'm not sure, but we could ask Barbara McCarthy. She's an expert on antiquarian books. Maybe old diaries fall into that category. But I want to read it first."

"Good idea."

Autumn stuffed the diary into her purse that was more like a tote bag. She needed to move into a smaller bag; the weight of this one pulled on her shoulder and made her neck stiff.

"Overall, I think this place is cool, but I don't know if I can picture myself living here. What do you think, Chrissy?"

She looked at Autumn and wagged her tail.

"Plenty of room for you to run around the house, little one. I'll need to get some rugs so you don't slide across the floor."

"This is a great place for Chrissy. Show it to Ray before making any decisions."

"Why should I show it to Ray?"

Stephanie waggled her eyebrows. "To see if he wants to live here with you."

"I don't know if *I* want to live here. Besides, we're definitely not at that stage yet!"

"He seems ready to me. You've always been a slow starter."

Autumn shook her head. "If that's true, then he can propose to me if he wants to live together."

"I can't see either of you with anyone else. You're too comfortable with each other."

Autumn smiled. Stephanie's assessment was true. Ray was easy to be around, and his acceptance of Autumn and Chrissy's needs was unconditional — at least so far. Her experience with her ex-boyfriend, Scott, showed that people could present themselves as one thing and then turn into something else. Her theory was at the six-month mark of their relationship, Ray would show himself to be the truly great guy he was now, or become self-absorbed the way Scott did. Autumn hoped beyond hope that she and Ray would go the distance and happily enter their senior years together.

She put Chrissy's leash back on and walked toward the door with Stephanie in tow. She locked up, and they walked around the house and past the museum entrance just as a woman came out. The large glasses perched on a beaked nose gave her an owlish appearance. A white rhinestone clip reminiscent of one of Chrissy's barrettes held the woman's wiry brown hair in place.

"What were you doing down there? This is private property," she snapped. "And no dogs allowed."

"May I ask your name?" said Autumn.

"Beatrice Peabody." She crossed her arms and stuck her nose in the air.

Autumn held out her hand. "I'm your cousin, Autumn Clarke. I'm happy to meet you."

"Excuse me?" Beatrice kept her arms locked.

Autumn put her hand down.

"I'm so sorry about Oxnard. He was a kind and generous man."

"No loss as far as I'm concerned. And how would you know anyway?"

"I was with him the day he died."

"You? Why were you there?"

"I was called at Oxnard's request. It seems we're related."

"What? I'm the last of our line!" Beatrice shrieked.

Chrissy backed away and shrunk down behind Autumn.

"Apparently not. Oxnard told me the family history, and I met with the attorney this morning. It came as quite a shock to me, as well."

"Why are you here?"

"Checking out my new house."

"Oh no you don't! If you think you're going to take this house out from under me, you're mistaken!"

Autumn stepped back to avoid the surge of nasty energy, the outburst like a toxic wind destroying any hope of having a relationship with Beatrice.

"Mr. Thornburg told me to have you give him a call. Here's his card."

Beatrice snatched the card from Autumn's hand, giving her a paper cut in the process.

"Ow," Autumn said and sucked blood from her finger.

"For all I know, you killed Oxnard to get the inheritance."

"I did no such thing! I didn't even know about it until Mr. Thornburg told me."

"I'll make sure you're locked up for Oxnard's murder!"

Beatrice turned and stomped off in a huff.

"That went well," said Stephanie.

"Ugh. This isn't what I hoped for."

"Let the attorney handle it. She's not someone you want to mess with."

"What if she accuses me of murder?"

"The lawyer knows that's not true, and so does Ray."

Autumn nodded.

"I thought she was going to hit me."

"Be careful. She's a nasty piece of work."

Chrissy squatted and put her two cents on the subject onto the spot where Beatrice had been standing.

C3 80

Beatrice held onto her anger until she approached her car. The gunmetal gray sedan with white leather interior made her feel like she was entering a coffin rather than a car. Her body was alive, but her soul had died along with her dream of living in the Peabody Mansion, dashed by a caveat in the will. She thought of Oxnard's body lying in the morgue at the medical examiner's office. She snarled thinking of their last conversation. He did tell her not to count on inheriting the mansion, but she dismissed him.

When the doctor called to say Oxnard was ill, it felt hypocritical to go to his bedside. She felt no grief or remorse for his pain and did not miss him or his advice. He grated on her nerves with his constant guidance about the Peabody Foundation, his criticism of her personality, and his disapproving glances.

Even her vision of leading the Peabody Foundation was misguided. The level of authority Oxnard commanded among the board members did not automatically transfer to her. Sitting in Oxnard's chair did not suit her the way she thought it would, the way it felt in her fantasies of taking over and being the last Peabody. The chair was too big, too hard to control suddenly rolling on its casters across the hard plastic mat underneath. The desk gave her a sense of Oxnard's ghost and the difficulties of the past rather than hope for the future. The authority she expected to wield from that vantage point did not fit her established persona. Beatrice sensed it with every staff member who entered Oxnard's office. They respected Oxnard's evenhanded governance but not her inherited authority. What was it about Oxnard that so easily commanded esteem?

Whenever she demanded something of Oxnard, he seemed to cower under her rage. Beatrice enjoyed putting Oxnard in his place, especially in front of others. She now recognized it was his self-control, tolerating her as the family decorum required. She realized her false sense of entitlement came across as immaturity to those who witnessed her abuses of her older brother. How did people see her now? Did they look upon her in pity as she floundered in Oxnard's shadow?

She vowed to show them that she truly had power. They underestimated her. It was a matter of acclimating to the role and of understanding her new responsibilities. Everyone would understand that she was now in charge, including Greg. His smug, condescending manner as he seduced her made her suspect of his motives. No other man gave her this type of attention. Her father had told her that the family name intimidated most men, along with her prominent nose, and big-boned physique. What made Greg different? Whatever they had together, she planned to remind him that she was boss.

Even Michael Thornburg disrespected her by withholding information about Autumn inheriting what Beatrice believed was rightfully hers. Beatrice resented Autumn muscling in on her turf. She could probably blow the woman across the parking lot with one breath, and her little dog along with her. She was an unexpected fly in the ointment, and she despised the idea of Autumn owning her family's mansion. She would give Michael Thornburg a piece of her mind and find out about this new twist in the inheritance.

⍥ **9** ⍥

Stephanie dropped Autumn and Chrissy off at home and left, promising not to do anything stupid regarding Greg. Autumn did not quite believe her, based on experience. She arranged for the locksmith to change the locks at Peabody Mansion and then called Ray to make plans for that evening. He and Ace would be over around six o'clock with dinner.

Autumn grabbed Chrissy's brush and scissors and spread a napkin on the floor in which to put the trimmed and brushed hair. She clicked the stereo remote and put on some soothing music. Her encounter with Beatrice rattled her nerves. With each stroke of the brush, Chrissy let out little grunts of pleasure and Autumn focused on her breathing. This ritual was comforting to both of them. She shared it with Dr. Wes, her psychiatrist, at their last session. He was pleased that she was finding creative ways to center herself, especially when they included Chrissy.

Her mind drifted to the Peabody Mansion, envisioning her sofa and loveseat positioned in the living room so that she and Chrissy could look out into the woods. She imagined Ray taking over the basement as his man-cave and hobby space. Next time she went to the house, she would bring him so they could check it out together. Chrissy flipped over and allowed Autumn to brush her tummy.

Autumn trimmed Chrissy's bangs and brushed her head, then pulled a wad of hair out of the brush and gave Chrissy hugs and kisses. Chrissy moaned in delight.

"My little darling," Autumn cooed.

Chrissy jumped up and shook off, her luxurious hair falling into place.

"One more thing."

Autumn pulled the hair away from Chrissy's eyes and twisted a cloth-coated pink and white polka dot elastic around it.

"You look beautiful!"

Chrissy smiled and trotted off to the kitchen for a drink of water.

Autumn wondered how Chrissy would like living in the stone mansion. It was close by, so she could still see her friends, but they wouldn't be on the street and at-the-ready for a walk. It would be a little more effort. This house was the only one Autumn had ever lived in. How would it feel to move? Would the mansion feel like her own or would history maintain its hold on the property? Besides, this house still felt like her parents' house, not as if it were Autumn's place.

Ace and Ray arrived on time carrying a large bag of Chinese food. Chrissy and Ace wagged tails and sniffed in greeting.

"What on earth did you order? It's only the two of us eating."

Ray kissed her and put the food on the counter.

"I decided to get the pupu platter, cashew shrimp for you, beef with broccoli for me, and some wonton soup to share."

Autumn laughed. "I hope you're hungry!"

"Trust me, nothing will go to waste." He looked at Chrissy.

"Somebody got brushed today!"

Chrissy wagged her tail at Ray.

Autumn fed the pups while Ray unpacked the bag.

"How was your day? Any exciting news from the coroner's office?"

"Actually, the toxicology report came back. The results are pretty interesting."

Autumn finished setting the table and waited. Ray smiled.

"You love teasing me, don't you?" She playfully punched him in the arm.

"Okay, Oxnard had traces of thallium in his system."

"What's thallium?"

"Good question. Thallium sulfate is actually a soft metal. The medical examiner had to do additional tests to confirm it. It makes you lose your hair, among other things."

"Oxnard's hair was all over his pillow when we visited him."

"The stuff is tasteless and odorless, so pinning down where he was exposed to it might be challenging."

Autumn ladled soup for each of them while Ray dug into the pupu platter.

"It was used as rat poison and a hair remover in the early 1900s."

"Where would someone get it now?"

"It's been prohibited in the United States since 1965 for household use, and commercially since 1975. The sad part is that there is an antidote called Prussian blue."

"Oxnard could have been saved if only he had gone to the hospital?"

"Yep."

Ray slurped a wonton. It made her think of the paper towel commercial where a wonton falls off the table and into the mouth of a waiting bulldog. If the news that they might have cured Oxnard did not weigh on her, she would have chuckled.

47

"I couldn't convince him to go." She poked at her shrimp without eating.

"It wasn't your fault. You tried. The crazy thing about this choice of poison is that its nicknames are 'the poisoner's poison' and 'inheritance powder' since it is hard to trace."

"Inheritance powder! Makes me think of Beatrice Peabody."

"Yes, it does."

Autumn put her fork down and took a breath.

"I ran into her today after meeting with Michael Thornburg, the Peabodys' lawyer."

Ray wiped his mouth and waited.

"Mr. Thornburg told me about my inheritance in detail and gave me the key to the mansion, so Stephanie, Chrissy, and I went to check it out. Greg Manning was there and confronted me about being on private property. When I told him I was the new owner, he claimed not to have known that Oxnard died. As we were leaving, Beatrice came out of the museum. When she found out the house is mine, she screamed at me and threatened to accuse me of murdering Oxnard. I referred her to Michael Thornburg, as he instructed."

She sighed.

"Right now Greg Manning and Beatrice Peabody are my top suspects in Oxnard's murder. I'd rather you didn't go back to the house alone."

"I was hoping you'd go with me. In the meantime, the locks are being changed tomorrow."

"That could antagonize them, so lie low. Greg's job is on the line and Beatrice may have killed for her inheritance."

"She didn't seem too upset that Oxnard died. In fact, she was indifferent when I gave her my condolences."

"I'll talk to both of them tomorrow. Please promise me you'll hang out around here for the next couple of days."

She squeezed his arm.

"I will."

Autumn got up and opened the sliding door for Chrissy and Ace. A blast of hot air from outside hit her and she knew the fur babies could not stay outside for long, so she waited. Sure enough, they came running back in after they did their business. They shook off the warmth and ran into the den toward Chrissy's toy pile. Autumn saw Chrissy pounce on her pink stuffed piggy while Ace grabbed the rope toy and shook it before settling down to gnaw on it. She rejoined Ray at the table.

"My little detective was hard at work while we were at the mansion. She found Abigail Peabody's diary. I plan to read it tomorrow."

"Does anyone else know you have it?"

"Just Stephanie."

"Please keep it that way for now."

"Okay. And I'll make sure Stephanie knows that, too."

"So many mysteries surround the Peabody family," said Ray, chewing bits of meat from the Chinese spareribs.

"Tell me about it. I'm still getting used to the idea of being one of them."

Ray ate the last spring roll dipped in duck sauce and patted his stomach.

"Did you say there's a good movie on television tonight?"

≈ 10 ≈

Julie Hall and Teddy the Yorkie came by the next morning. Autumn made coffee while Chrissy played ball with Teddy in the den.

"Brad was shocked at Chrissy's discovery," said Julie.

"I think we all were. Who expects a hand to be sticking out of the ground in the middle of a festival?"

"Or anywhere, really." Julie poured cream in her coffee.

"Thousands of people, including us, have walked over that body for years. It's creepy when you think about it."

"We know the skeleton dates back to around 1935."

"So it could be Abigail."

"Possibly. Some DNA comparisons would be nice. Maybe Beatrice Peabody would cooperate."

Autumn hesitated at the suggestion. She was obligated to keep the secret of Beatrice's lineage.

"Oxnard Peabody is a better choice."

"He would definitely be more cooperative."

Autumn's face scrunched in sadness.

"Sorry, bad joke. Yes, we can take it from Oxnard."

"Let me tell Ray. I'll just be a moment."

"Of course."

Autumn dialed Ray and left a message about the skeleton and the needed DNA. She tapped her fingers on the table. Maybe the diary held clues to the identity of the skeleton.

"Chrissy!"

Chrissy came running into the kitchen, Teddy on her heels.

"A walk will help us to think," said Autumn, "before it gets too hot out."

"Yes, right now it's only in the mid-eighties." Julie fanned herself.

They put harnesses on the pups and the group set off down the street.

⁂

Sweating from the walk, Autumn ran a brush over Chrissy and then jumped in the shower. Clean and cool, she grabbed the diary and got comfortable in her favorite spot in the library window seat where the light was perfect to see the aged pages. Chrissy decided that it was cooler on the floor and stretched out on her side.

Autumn ran her fingers over the scratched brown leather cover and traced the embossed rose design with her nail. She opened the book, hearing the spine crack. Abigail's name written on the bookplate in a looped script extended above and below the line. It had an artistic flair. She wondered if Abigail was killed before she could conceal the diary. On the other hand, was it hidden and had the killer had found it? Either way, finding it on the floor in the den meant someone else had recently read it.

She carefully turned to the first entry page. The date was November 15, 1934, less than a year before her disappearance. Autumn started reading and lost herself in Abigail's fear and melancholy.

Autumn's horror grew as she read account after account of Great-Grandfather Horatio's criticism of everything Abigail did in front of the staff, family, and friends. Her heart broke for Abigail with every discovered infidelity. His tastes ran the gamut from their own household staff to the wives of Horatio's business associates.

The worst was when Horatio had admitted being in love with Daphne Clarke and that she was pregnant. Abigail wrote that she suspected Horatio and Daphne of planning to do away with her so they could be together.

When Abigail's hair started falling out, she tried a wig, but eventually withdrew from public life and kept to her room more and more. To think she was of Horatio's bloodline disturbed Autumn. The Clarke family had more care and compassion for others in their actions and relationships. Now that she knew the truth, would she notice tendencies of her own moving away from the Clarke mindset and into the brutality of the Peabody way? She saw it in Beatrice, but not so much in Oxnard. Beatrice had only her mother's lineage to blame it on. Oxnard was a full-fledged Peabody. There was a chance that nurture would win over nature.

Besides the philanthropic nature of Autumn's mother and her father's kindness was bound to win out over Horatio's indiscretions two generations removed.

The sun shone through the windows moving shadows from the mullions across Autumn. She sat perfectly still, absorbed in the trials of a marriage to Horatio Peabody, Abigail's pain apparent on every page.

Chrissy growled and waited. Getting no response, she growled again. This time, her efforts paid off, pulling Autumn back from the past. She blinked and met Chrissy's clear, dark eyes.

"What is it, sweetheart?

Chrissy growled and then let out one sharp bark.

"Show me."

Chrissy trotted into the kitchen with Autumn behind her. She walked to her water bowl and sat down.

"No water! Let me get you some right now."

Autumn wiped out the bowl, filled it with filtered water, and topped it with one ice cube. Chrissy looked up at her and smiled, then lapped up the cool drink. Autumn looked at the clock. It was almost one o'clock. She put her hand to her head. Her fascination with Abigail's difficult journey provided information about her state of mind and Great-Grandfather Horatio's alcoholism. The idea that she was reading about her own family history never escaped her. She wished she could talk to her father about all of this.

She made herself a sandwich and gave Chrissy a snack. She ate quickly while watching Chrissy enjoy her treat. Autumn was eager to return to what was now 1935 in the chronicle, where a forty-five-year-old Abigail poured her heartbreak and dread into the diary. Autumn hoped to discover more about the body in the park and Abigail's own disappearance. She and Chrissy went back into the library room and got comfortable on the window seat. Chrissy positioned herself between Autumn's legs, her head on Autumn thigh for the best view of the yard. A squirrel jumped onto the tree in front of the window, and Chrissy grunted at it.

Autumn picked up the diary and noticed a dog-eared page. It puzzled her, since the book included multiple ribbon markers for place holding. Her deep love of books prompted an extensive collection of bookmarkers, and the dog-eared page offended her. She opened to the folded page to straighten the dismaying fold and a postcard slipped out and fell to the floor.

Written in a straighter hand than Abigail's, it showed an illustration of the Hudson River Valley in New York, a blank space where a note should be, and Abigail's Knollwood address.

Autumn thought about Barbara McCarthy's expertise and decided to go over to her shop to see what she thought. Her promise to Ray weighed on her. She had to wait until he gave permission to proceed, so she gave him a call and got his voicemail. Hearing his voice made her smile. She left a message for him to call her. In the meantime, she kept reading.

CB80

Greg Manning finished trimming the shrubs near the museum entrance, sweat dripping down his face. Summer heat made his outdoor work harder. He put his tools in the shed and locked the door, deciding he would rather work indoors today. He wondered what the change in ownership meant for his livelihood.

He walked around to the residence front door and tried inserting his key, but it no longer fit. Grumbling, he backtracked to the museum.

Entering the gift shop, he helped himself to a bottle of cold water, held it up to Darlene, the new girl at the counter, who nodded, and then he chugged it down. He wiped his mouth with the back of his hand.

"Hot out there," said Darlene.

"You're telling me. Have you seen Beatrice around?"

"She's upstairs in the office."

Greg waved and mounted the stairs.

He knocked at the thick wooden door that used to be Oxnard's office.

"Come in!"

Seeing Beatrice behind Oxnard's desk gave him a pang of regret. She looked up, her normally stern gaze softening.

"What can I do for you?"

"I met the new owner."

Beatrice's face crumpled, brows furrowed, and her mouth twisted in disgust.

"I called the attorney. Seems my distant relatives made sure I didn't get the house. And I found out he confirmed that the woman with the dog is truly my cousin. I just got rid of one relative; what do I need with another one?"

"How is that possible?"

"Great-Grandfather Horatio liked to spread his seed around and one of his plantings took."

"Any chance of contesting the heredity?"

"No. It's been verified by every generation — part of the family history that Oxnard kept from me."

"She changed the lock on the residence."

"If you're worried about your job here, you're safe at the museum as long as I'm here. For the mansion, I can't say."

Greg moved closer to the desk.

"How does this affect us?"

Beatrice leaned back in the executive chair, her authority lacking. She was no Oxnard Peabody.

"You tell me."

Greg came alongside the desk and leaned over Beatrice, her face lifting to meet his.

"This is an unexpected stroke of luck," said Ray Reed from the open doorway.

They quickly pulled back as if they were kids caught making out in the back seat of a car.

"Detective," said Greg.

Beatrice folded her arms.

"I'd appreciate it if you could answer some questions."

"I'm not required to do anything of the sort," said Beatrice.

"It's completely voluntary, Ms. Peabody. I'm just gathering information."

"About what?" Greg took a protective stance next to Beatrice.

"May I sit down?"

Beatrice pointed to an armchair in front of the desk.

Ray opened his notepad.

"We are running tests on the body found at the festival. Any idea who it might be?"

"I've mowed that field more times than I can count over the last twenty years and never saw anything out of the ordinary. Makes me think that it was buried before I got here."

"What about you, Ms. Peabody? Anything that might shed some light on this?"

"No."

"I understand your great-grandmother Abigail went missing in 1935. Any chance it could be her?"

"I don't know. I never heard anything about it except that she left to go see relatives in upstate New York and never arrived."

Greg saw Beatrice fidgeting. He could tell that the detective made her uncomfortable.

"What about your brother?

"What about him?"

"Any idea what made him sick?"

"No idea."

"Did either of you observe his movements during the day?"

"I saw him in the dunking booth. People loved soaking him," said Greg.

"And after that?"

"The body was found, so he got out of the tank and we closed it up for the night and drained it in the morning. I saw him get into his car after talking to you."

"Either of you know about Jasper Wiggins being fired at the festival? Oxnard was overheard accusing someone of drinking on the job."

"No, but Oxnard warned Jasper about his drinking more than once," said Beatrice.

"When was the last time you saw Mr. Wiggins?"

"The last time I visited Oxnard, sometime last week."

"How about you, Mr. Manning? Have you been in contact with Mr. Wiggins?"

"Now that you mention it, no. I haven't seen him since the festival."

"When was the last time you saw him?"

"Right before Oxnard got into the dunking booth."

"If either of you see him, would you please ask him to call me? Or think of anything that might be useful, can you please call me?"

Ray closed his notebook and handed them each a card.

"Thanks for your time."

They watched him leave and looked at each other. Greg smiled and leaned toward Beatrice.

"Now where were we?"

Cঙৎ০

Autumn was deep into Abigail's diary when the sun dipped behind dark clouds and the first roll of thunder blasted through the sky. Chrissy shook, looking at Autumn in panic. Putting the book down, she grabbed her little girl, holding her tight against her chest and went into the living room. They snuggled in a big chair away from the window. At another clap of thunder and the first drops of rain, Chrissy went into full shaking mode. Autumn whispered in her ear and tried distracting her with a squeaky toy, but consoling Chrissy during a storm was challenging. There was no soundproof room to block the sounds of the storm like at the Peabody Mansion.

Autumn rocked her and wrapped a blanket around Chrissy's ears to dull the sounds of the storm. Her phone rang, and she answered with one hand while holding Chrissy tight with the other.

"Hey, babe," said Ray, "what are you doing?"

"Hi. I'm trying to calm Chrissy. The storm sent her into full panic."

"It came on suddenly. I got caught in it as I was leaving the Peabody Museum."

"Did you find out anything?"

"They were reluctant, but I confirmed that Jasper Wiggins has a drinking problem."

"When I was there, I didn't see anyone else. I'd think that he would be helping Oxnard in such a critical situation."

"Not if Oxnard fired him. Neither Greg nor Beatrice has seen him since the festival. I need to find out where he his."

"Listen, Chrissy is terrified. I need to go."

"I'll come over later with Ace."

She hung up, put on some peaceful instrumental music, and grabbed Chrissy's brush. Chrissy pressed against her, tremors moving through her little body. Autumn kissed Chrissy's fuzzy head while gently brushing her. It seemed to quell the shivers and helped them both relax. Since Chrissy came into her life, Autumn had had very few panic attacks. Focusing on the needs of this little girl shifted her mind away from her own troubles and grief. Autumn had become Chrissy's emotional-support human, which was a nice change from the other way around.

They stayed in the chair until the storm passed and the sun beamed through a crystal pyramid sitting on the coffee table, making prisms on the floor. Chrissy leaped from the chair, shaking off once she hit the floor. She smiled up at Autumn and trotted into the kitchen for a drink of water. Autumn decided to try shaking her head and body when coming out of her own panic mode to clear any remnants of the experience.

Chrissy barked before Autumn heard the knock on the door. She opened it to find Steve Coleman and Mickey. The heat came in with them even though the storm reduced the humidity. The standard poodle walked in and brushed against Chrissy on his way to the kitchen to look for a snack. Chrissy ran after him, her shorter legs doing triple time over the poodle's long strides.

Autumn was happy to live in a community where neighbors felt free to stop by with their pets, and Chrissy enjoyed the impromptu walks.

"Some storm! How did Chrissy make out?"

"The usual. We have a routine now to manage the panic, but it breaks my heart to see her go through it. I know how it feels."

Steve patted her shoulder. "I know you do."

The pups came back to the foyer.

"Want to take a walk with Mickey?" Autumn asked Chrissy.

Chrissy wagged her tail and stepped into her black, rolled-leather harness. They took their usual route around the neighborhood,

Chrissy's feet getting soaked despite Autumn lifting her over the deep puddles. Along the way, she kept conversation light. She wanted to share her news but needed more time to sit with it herself before sharing it more broadly.

11

When Ray and Ace arrived, dinner was in the oven. Autumn let Chrissy and Ace play for a while before feeding them. Chrissy's appetite grew after playing, so she was more likely to eat all of her food.

"How was your day?"

"Interesting. I think Greg and Beatrice are an item."

"What makes you say that?"

"I caught them in her office, faces almost touching. They jumped apart when I came to the door. It was all I could do not to laugh."

"Uh oh."

"What?"

"Stephanie likes Greg. She's been flirting with him—unsuccessfully, I might add."

"Probably not the best idea. I still don't know what part he's playing in all of this."

"The good news is he ignored her when we were with him at the mansion."

"Has he tried to contact you since you changed the locks?"

"Nope. I'm not looking forward to that conversation, although I don't see a reason not to let him continue with the landscaping."

"Maybe. Plus, that would let me keep an eye on him. But I don't want you alone with him."

"I want to go back into the mansion and look for clues about Abigail and whether she's the body in the park."

"I'll go with you. Let's go tomorrow. How are you making out with the journal?"

"I'm still reading, but a postcard sent to Abigail Peabody slipped out of it. It was sent from upstate New York."

"Isn't that where she supposedly went when she disappeared?"

"Yes. I don't blame her for leaving. Horatio was an emotionally abusive, philandering drunkard. I'm surprised she stayed as long as she did."

"Divorce wasn't as common back then as it is today."

"It's dismaying to think I'm part of his gene pool."

"Balanced by Daphne Clarke's. I've been with you for four months and only see how loving and caring you are. Tell me now if you think you'll turn into an alcoholic Peabody monster at some point."

Autumn chuckled. "Doubtful."

"Exactly. Now, what smells so good?"

⚮

Autumn pointed the way to the mansion's driveway. Ray parked his SUV, and they released the seatbelts holding Chrissy and Ace snugly in the backseat. Chrissy liked sitting with Ace when he was in the car. They both shook off and trotted up to the massive front door, Chrissy's body joyfully rolling side-to-side while Ace's solid stride maintained his guard-dog image.

"There are a couple of scratches on the key plate. I'll bet Greg tried to get in with his old key."

Autumn pulled out her key and slid it into the brand new lock. Cool air escaped the foyer and the four of them entered.

"Wow."

"I know, right?"

Autumn locked the door behind them. Ace and Chrissy would probably sound the alarm if someone tried to get in, but the house was practically soundproof, and she did not want anybody sneaking in while she and Ray were in another part of the house.

They walked slowly through each room, Autumn noticing more details than the first time through, and Ray admiring the woodwork and leaded-glass windows. They climbed the wide wooden staircase to the second floor.

"Can you see Chrissy and me living here?"

"What are you going to do with eight bedrooms?"

"Make that ten bedrooms. Maybe I should turn it into a boarding house."

Ray had not taken the bait. She had hoped he would hint that the space would be better if he and Ace moved in here, too.

Back downstairs, Chrissy sniffed around the fireplace and along the bookcase in the den.

"Here's where Chrissy found the diary."

She pointed to the chair and recreated the diary's position using a book from the shelf.

"Someone else may have known about the diary," Autumn offered. "It's an odd place to find it. I doubt it's been there since Abigail disappeared. If she were leaving forever, I'd expect she'd want to take it and not leave it behind for Horatio to discover."

"Or for anyone else to find it. Not everyone knew that Daphne was pregnant with Horatio's baby. Unless Horatio murdered her after he found the diary. But I agree that with Greg, Oxnard, and probably Beatrice in and out of here, someone must have been reading it."

Autumn led Ray to the basement door. She opened it and flicked the light switch, illuminating the room at the base of the stairway. Ace and Chrissy came running and charged down the stairs.

"I don't want her down there alone!" cried Autumn.

Autumn ran down the steps with Ray right behind her. At the bottom, the dingy basement held boxes of unknown treasures and lots of dust and dirt. Empty glass bottles of blue and green decorated shelves along the walls.

"Chrissy!"

She came running, tail wagging.

"That's my good girl. Stay with Mommy."

She did. Ace sniffed the vicinity within sight of Ray.

"This is some basement."

"If I move in here, can you think of a use for it?"

"With the eight-foot ceilings, you could do anything down here."

"Pool table, ping pong, maybe a movie theater?"

"A bowling alley?"

They both laughed.

Walking into the next room of the cavernous basement, they saw piles of books and glassware along the walls. Autumn pulled one of the volumes off the stack and discovered it was a photo album. Paging through, she recognized photos of Horatio Peabody. His face was a regular decoration for the annual Peabody Festival. She wanted to know who the other people in the photos were. Digging through the pile, she found two more photo albums and carried them closer to the stairs.

"I wonder if Barbara McCarthy would come down here and appraise these books."

"I'm sure she would. That's her passion in life, right?" Ray replied.

"Right!" said Autumn.

Ray explored the other side of the room and found corked bottles in a wooden box. He read the labels and saw that they were rat poison.

"Looky here! A case of thallium."

Autumn came over and Chrissy followed. Autumn scooped Chrissy off the floor before she had a chance to sniff the bottles. She also grabbed Ace by the collar and kept him back.

"That isn't good for babies," she said and kissed Chrissy.

"Now we know where the poison used on Oxnard came from."

"That narrows it down to the people who had access to this building."

"Like Greg, for example. He could have let Beatrice in, as well."

"Maybe even Jasper Wiggins."

Ray nodded. "I'll be right back."

He returned with a camera, plastic gloves, a large plastic evidence bag, and an evidence tag. He snapped a few photos of the area and the case of poison. After bagging and tagging the box to preserve fingerprints and other potential evidence, he carefully transported it to his truck and then went back down to the basement. They finished walking through the remaining rooms down there, each loaded with boxes, furniture, and random decorative items.

"This is going to be one major clean-up project," said Autumn.

"I'll help you, and we can get one of those charities that take donations to come get anything that's salvageable."

"Maybe there are some valuable antiques."

"Possibly. Most of this stuff would seem out of place except in a house like this one."

Autumn nodded, trying to formulate the plan to get it done. She trusted that a one-room-at-a-time plan starting with the farthest room from the steps would work best. Recruiting Stephanie to stay upstairs with the pups was also part of her strategy. The basement was a dangerous place for curious canines and probably for humans, as well.

"Let's get going. I want to get those bottles to the lab. We can come back on Saturday."

Autumn grabbed the photo albums and encouraged Chrissy and Ace to scoot up the stairs in front of her.

⋘⋙

Ray dropped off Autumn and Chrissy at home and went straight to the lab with his newfound evidence. Autumn removed Chrissy's harness and then put down a bowl of fresh water. Chrissy took a long drink before Autumn hauled her out to the patio for a good brushing. Lord only knew what might have gotten onto her coat in that filthy basement. Back inside, Autumn wiped down the covers of the photo albums with a damp paper towel with Chrissy nestled under the kitchen table.

Autumn leafed through the book. Old photos had a way of making people look older than they actually were. Even children seemed like they were in their twenties. She booted up her laptop, searched for images of Abigail Peabody, found a few, and then compared them to the photographs in the albums. She recognized Abigail and using the dates scratched onto each page saw her mood diminish, from the earliest pictures of her smiling next to Horatio to a turned down mouth and shoulders hiked up to her jaw with stress in later photos. It was a timeline of Horatio Peabody's effect on poor Abigail, consistent with the diary.

Even more startling was the gradual hair loss that became noticeable in the later shots. Patches of scalp showed through Abigail's thinning hair. The grainy black-and-white photos did not allow a determination of pallor, but Autumn guessed it was similar to Oxnard's yellow tint before his death. The only conclusion was that Horatio Peabody, or someone else close to her, gradually poisoned her with thallium, given the hair loss. In subsequent pictures, Abigail wore a wig. She probably never actually left Knollwood to visit the idyllic Hudson River Valley depicted on the postcard.

Great-Grandfather Horatio's smug look annoyed Autumn. Sometimes his pose demonstrated his standing in the community, with one hand wrapped around the lapel of his thick jacket. Other times his expression was lascivious, especially when he had Abigail on his right and another woman on his left, Horatio's hand squeezing the unknown woman's shoulder.

There were pictures of Horatio and Abigail with their son, Maynard, as an infant, soon after his birth in 1904 and others of Maynard through his twenties. His mother disappeared when he was thirty-one; and afterward, the photos showed only Maynard Peabody and his father. They looked worn and detached. For all of their wealth, this family seemed full of dismay as though waiting for something terrible to happen. It could be the photographic style of the time since most vintage photos showed people with sullen faces. But then again, the mood of the family members shifted over time.

What bothered Autumn was the unknown female pictured next to Abigail. Maybe there was something in the diary about her.

ᏃᏇᏁ

Stephanie loved shopping on Main Street. She enjoyed seeing the shop owners' creativity with windows decorated to entice shoppers to come in and browse. Jade's Jewelry had one of the best window displays. The glittering pieces mesmerized Stephanie, but the prices brought her back to reality. She waved to long-time residents of Knollwood, many of whom were parents to her students. They reminded her to cut short her favorite sport of window-shopping and focus on her mission to find engaging decorations for the bulletin board in her classroom. Jansen's Stationary on the corner of Main and Pine had the best selection of borders and colored paper.

A block away from her destination, Stephanie spotted Greg Manning strutting down the street. She watched him enter Attic Treasures Books and saw an opportunity to reintroduce herself. She took her time and gazed into the Knitique clothing shop window before crossing the street and entering the bookstore. The smell of old books made her smile. She ran her hand over a table loaded with hardcover art books, some from the late 1800s.

Mumbling in the back of the store caught her attention and she worked her way to the employees-only area. Moans replaced the mumbling and Stephanie stifled a gasp at the shocking vision of Barbara pushed against the wall and Greg kissing her deeply. No wonder he had ignored her at the mansion. Stephanie made a beeline for the exit before either of them saw her.

Outside, Stephanie stomped her foot, stunned that Greg Manning found Barbara McCarthy attractive. How long had the relationship been going on? No one talked about it, and in this closely-knit community, people knew who was with whom. With a deep sigh, she pushed on to finish her errand.

ⒸⒼⓈⓄ

Autumn and Chrissy snuggled on the window seat. The deeper she read into the diary, the more she felt Abigail's worsening mood and ill health. Horatio's many affairs, including with the household staff, troubled her. She also suspected that her hair loss was the result of some sort of poison. She wrote that she ate and drank only what she prepared herself. She trusted no one. Abigail's diminished state of health apparently lowered her ability to hide her feelings. The filter came off and her words spewed hate onto the yellowed pages. Abigail wrote that she hid the journal, fearing Horatio's wrath, alternating between putting it under the mattress and under a loose board in the closet floor. Autumn made a note to check those places for other clues.

If Abigail generally hid the diary, how did it end up in the sitting room by a chair? Ray's comment that someone had been reading the diary before she found it gnawed at her.

Tension built as she read what Abigail went through, so Autumn stopped reading to pet Chrissy. Chrissy grunted with pleasure. She wondered if the postcard was an attempt by the family to get Abigail to join them in the Hudson River Valley. Rejoining her family may have been the only way to escape a horrific marriage. She wanted to know who had sent the postcard and needed to dig into Abigail's family history. Maybe Barbara McCarthy at Attic Treasures Books could help with her knowledge of local folklore.

⋐⋑

Ray stood over the lab technician as he ran the tests on the bottles of thallium, both of them wearing masks and gloves. Ace sat near the door a safe distance from the toxic substance.

"Some prints are nice and clear. Others are smudged as though the person handling these bottles handled another layer on top of this one, so the fingers grazed the bottles in this carton when he picked up the one above it. My guess is that there was another crate of thallium and this is the rest of it."

"Could some of the prints belong to another person?"

"The width variation of the smudged prints might indicate a second person handling the bottles, but it's inconclusive."

"Is the potency enough to kill someone?"

"Oh, yeah. This stuff is dangerous, especially if you don't have the antidote, Prussian Blue, nearby in case of exposure. There's no taste, no odor. It's water-soluble making it versatile as a murder weapon. "

"That would make it ideal for something like a dunking tank."

The lab tech nodded in agreement. "There was likely enough thallium in the missing crate to ensure the right potency to do the job."

Ray thought of Chrissy going near it and was grateful she did not get any on her. They did not have the antidote with them if something had happened. He also felt sad for Oxnard's unnecessary death. It made him believe that the murderer did not know that Oxnard could recover from the poison.

"Do we have an ID on the prints?"

"Gregory Manning. We have his prints from a DUI arrest a few years back."

64

"Good. One more thing. Take a sample of DNA from Oxnard. I'd like his sample compared with that of the skeleton we found in the park."

"I'll let you know as soon as we have the results."

Ray thanked the tech. He realized that as the caretaker of Peabody Mansion, Greg might have used the thallium as rat poison, so he could not make an arrest based on Greg Manning's fingerprints alone. He needed to find out about one more person and left to talk to Michael Thornburg. His office was a few blocks from the police station, so he and Ace walked. The attorney was welcoming.

"What can I do for you Detective Reed?"

"Do you know anything about Jasper Wiggins?"

"Of course. He was Oxnard's house manager."

"What does a house manager do?"

"Mr. Wiggins managed Oxnard's calendars and schedules, made appointments, dealt with contractors and home repairs, and paid bills, among other things."

"Are Oxnard's accounts in order? Any money missing?"

"Are you implying that Wiggins stole money and took off?"

"All possibilities are open right now."

"I'll check into the finances, just to make sure."

"Have you seen him since Mr. Peabody passed away?"

"Come to think of it, I haven't."

"Where does he live? Can you provide me with the address?"

"He lived with Oxnard. I was at the house when Oxnard fell ill, but didn't see Wiggins at all. Oxnard said he fired him at the festival, which would explain why he wasn't around."

"Thank you, Mr. Thornburg. I'll be in touch."

Ray Reed left wondering if Jasper Wiggins was involved in Oxnard's death. Oxnard fell ill after Autumn had overheard him firing Wiggins. It was still only circumstantial to assume that Wiggins was involved, since he had disappeared. But Jasper Wiggins was in the top three suspects, which included Beatrice Peabody and Greg Manning.

They all had motive and opportunity. Beatrice wanted the Peabody Mansion and did not know about the technicalities that prevented her from inheriting it. Greg's likely affair with Beatrice may have motivated him to act against Oxnard for her, or for reasons not yet known. Jasper's firing may have resulted in revenge. All of them could access the thallium in the basement of the Peabody mansion. All of them were at the Peabody Festival and had access to the dunk tank. That was the most likely place of Oxnard's exposure to the poison, since the onset of his illness occurred after his repeated dunking. It was also possible that any one of them snuck some thallium sulfate into Oxnard's food or drink over time. The cumulative effect could have killed him.

Ray and Ace got into the SUV and drove over to Oxnard's house. The grounds were magnificent. A late model red sports car was in the driveway next to Beatrice Peabody's gunmetal gray luxury car. Ray and Ace approached the front door and rang the bell. Beatrice answered. She glowered at the detective.

"Good afternoon Ms. Peabody. May I come in?"

"What do you want?"

"I'd like to examine Jasper Wiggins room, if you don't mind."

"I do mind. This is my house now."

"A beautiful home it is, too. The grounds are amazing."

Beatrice Peabody continued blocking the doorway and did not speak.

"I'd rather not get a search warrant, Ms. Peabody. Besides, depending on what happened to Mr. Wiggins, you might be exonerated."

"Of what?"

"Your brother's murder, of course."

Her hands clenched and pounded the side of her leg.

"He was ill, detective."

"He was poisoned, Ms. Peabody."

Ray watched her eyes momentarily widen, then go back to her normal.

"I just want to see Jasper Wiggins' room, and then I'll leave you to enjoy your new home."

She squinted at him, frowned at Ace, and then stepped back from the door to let him in.

"Up the stairs, second door on the right."

"Thank you."

Ray and Ace climbed the steps. A stair runner over the honey-colored hardwood treads made climbing the stairs easier for Ace. Family portraits lined the walls. He recognized Oxnard and Beatrice as adults, and Great-Grandfather Horatio. One photo showed the siblings as children with their parents, Edgar and Mary. Ray recognized the same dour expressions in youth as they had as adults.

The creamy white upstairs hallway had honey maple wainscoting along the bottom and a massive arched window. Some of the panes incorporated stained-glass fleur-de-lis in shades of green and blue. The landing curved around to a longer hallway. The second door on the right was at the opposite end from what Ray assumed was the master bedroom with its wide double doors and gold doorknobs. He found Wiggins's door ajar, and he pushed it open. Ace instinctively stayed back and guarded the doorway.

The brocade bedspread punctuated with coordinating decorative pillows lay perfectly flat, made as though no one had ever slept there. A jacket neatly hung on a wooden stand. All surfaces were free of dust and clutter. The closet was full of suits and shoes. Ray noticed a suitcase tucked into the corner of the closet. In the attached bath, a toothbrush and shaving kit sat on the counter. Jasper had not left town. So where was he?

Ray and Ace went back downstairs.

"Ms. Peabody, it looks like Mr. Wiggins still lives in that room. All of his things are still there."

"I don't know what to tell you."

"Have you seen him at any time since the festival?"

"No."

"By any chance, do you have a photograph of Mr. Wiggins?"

"No."

"You have my card in case a photo or Mr. Wiggins turns up."

Beatrice gave a single nod and walked away. Ray let himself out.

12

Autumn balanced the phone against her shoulder while trying to brush sticks and yard debris from their morning walk out of Chrissy's hair. Chrissy's short little legs put her close to the ground and the long hair attracted burs and debris from plants growing wild near the sidewalk. Mickey's height spared him from the same fate. He was tall enough that Chrissy could walk under him if she felt the urge to take a shortcut across the sidewalk.

"Am I allowed out of the neighborhood now?" she asked Ray.

"I'll be tracking down Greg today, so you should be okay. Just stay alert."

"I have the best furry alarm system on the market. She'll make sure I don't miss anything."

Ray laughed. "I'll call you later."

Autumn put down the phone and finished Chrissy's morning groom. She ate cereal while reading the last few pages of the diary, being careful not to splash milk on the pages.

The entry read: I can't wait any longer. I must—

Autumn gasped, making Chrissy jump and look up at Autumn.

"It's okay, sweetheart." She petted Chrissy's head, assuring her everything was fine. Chrissy settled back down under the kitchen table.

The last page was missing. There was a remnant of the ripped leaf in the crevice of the binding.

Autumn closed the diary and set it aside, wondering why Abigail had not taken the whole diary with her. Why just the last page? She had probably packed in a hurry, desperate to get away from Horatio. Autumn focused on her breath trying to relax her body. She stood up and paced the living room. Was the woman buried on the festival grounds Abigail or someone else? Did Horatio tear out the page or did Abigail? Or did someone else tear it out, possibly whoever found and read the diary before Autumn?

She had lots to discuss with Dr. Wes at her appointment later on. First, she wanted to visit Attic Treasures to see what she could learn.

കൃട്

Chrissy's hips swayed and her tail swished back and forth as they walked down the sidewalk toward the bookshop. Colorful end-of-summer and back-to-school sales banners were in many of the shop windows. Yellow and green streamers decorated the book display outside Barbara McCarthy's shop. Lit by early afternoon sun, it drew Autumn's attention to the featured books, several of which Autumn was eager to read. A cart loaded with hardback books and a clearance sign tantalized her to pick through the pile; she found two volumes to buy.

Chrissy walked in first to the sound of a small bell on the door. It was cool and dim inside the shop to protect the books, both old and new, from deterioration and fading. Bookcases lined the walls and formed aisles in the middle of the store. Chrissy sniffed at a table leg of the round book display at the front of the shop holding large volumes of art and nature photography. She sneezed dust from her nose and shook her entire body. Autumn watched to see if her bow flew off, but it stayed in place.

A door banged shut somewhere in the back of the building. Barbara McCarthy came out of the employee area, smoothing her hair and tucking in her shirt.

"Hi, Autumn," Barbara said bending down to pet Chrissy. "Hello there you silky fur baby."

"Hi, Barbara. I found these out front."

"It's hard to resist a clearance cart of books. Come over to the counter."

"Don't ring me up just yet. I hope you can help me with information about town folklore."

"It's my favorite topic. Let's sit back here."

Barbara led Autumn and Chrissy to a comfortable nook with floor lamps and small tables next to upholstered reading chairs. They each took a seat and Chrissy made herself comfortable on the area rug at Autumn's feet.

"Ever since the body was found in the park, the Peabody family history is of interest to me," said Autumn. She cringed at the lie, but she was not yet certain whom to trust with her new Peabody status. "I'm hoping you have information about what happened to Abigail Peabody."

"The story goes that she went to the train station and headed to upstate New York to visit relatives. Her relatives say she never made it up there. No one ever heard from her again. Horatio Peabody donated the land we use for the Peabody festival soon after her disappearance."

"Do you think she met with foul play?"

"It's hard to say. I guess the skeleton Chrissy found will tell us that. It's a shame that Abigail lived in the shadow of Horatio Peabody. I'd like to know more about her. Most of the written history is about him. Quite the ladies' man from all accounts."

Autumn's thoughts turned to the details in the diary. Seeing that journal would be a dream come true for Barbara.

"Do you know anything about his affairs?"

"He did not discriminate between married or unmarried. Since he had business dealings with most of the men in Knollwood and they relied on him to earn a living, Horatio felt their wives were at his disposal."

"What about his staff?"

"He employed a staff of ten men and women to care for the Peabody Mansion, himself, and his wife, Abigail."

The bell tinkled and a customer walked in and got lost in the stacks. Chrissy watched him walk in and let out a low growl. She peered in his direction for a minute, growling some more. With a lack of action on Autumn's part, she decided there was nothing to see and put her head back on her fluffy white paws. Autumn reached down and petted her head.

"Could there have been any hanky-panky going on with the staff?"

"Most likely. Horatio was a powerful man and took what he wanted."

"Do you have the names of his staff?"

"Over the years, there was turnover. Many of them could only deal with Horatio and his demands for so long before they moved on. Their pay was high for the house staff roles at the time, but their tolerance was low."

"Did the women stay?"

Barbara hesitated.

"It depended on the woman."

Autumn pulled out the photo album from her carryall and turned to the picture with Horatio, Abigail, and the unknown woman. She showed it to Barbara and pointed to the woman.

"How about this woman? Any idea whom she might be?"

Autumn watched Barbara's eyes widen for a split second then caught herself.

"Hmmm. I'd have to do some research."

"I'd like to know if she's a member of the staff or of the family."

"I'll go through my archives and see if I can find anything about her."

Barbara pressed her lips together, snapped a shot of the photo with her cell phone, and handed the album back to Autumn.

"Where did the album come from?"

Autumn was not prepared to answer questions like that.

"Uh, I found it in the basement of the Peabody Mansion."

Barbara squinted.

"There have been rumors about your family and the Peabody clan for years, in particular a love affair between Horatio Peabody and Daphne Clarke. Are you related?"

Autumn hesitated, and then realized it would come out eventually.

"I recently found out that I'm Oxnard and Beatrice's cousin. Please keep that to yourself for now."

Barbara nodded.

"I keep more secrets about the people in this town than you can imagine."

Autumn pointed to the photo album.

"I appreciate any info you can come up with."

Barbara stood, signaling the end of their meeting.

She walked Autumn to the counter, completed her purchase, and asked her to fill out a work order with her contact information.

"My research fee is fifty dollars an hour. I'll call you whether or not I find anything."

Autumn nodded in agreement as she tucked her new books into the tote. It made sense to pay Barbara for her time. She waved to a stone-faced Barbara as she led Chrissy toward the door. Chrissy stopped to check out the back of the man still browsing the stacks in the cook-book section.

"Come on, Chrissy. We have one more stop to make before we head home."

Chrissy stood her ground.

"You want to say hello?"

Chrissy walked over to the man.

"She wants to say hi."

The dark-haired man turned around.

"Oh, Greg!"

His energy made her body tense up. She hoped nothing would come of Stephanie's pursuit of his affection. Chrissy sat. Greg made no move to pet her and scowled at Autumn.

"You changed the locks."

"Yes."

"Am I fired?"

71

"I'd like to have a meeting to go over your duties. Are you available tomorrow? I know it's Saturday, so we could wait until Monday if—"

"The sooner the better. I want to know where I stand."

"Let's say one o'clock tomorrow afternoon. We can meet at the mansion."

He gave a curt nod.

"See you then," said Autumn and tugged Chrissy to walk with her. She was glad to hear the door close behind her, putting a barrier between them.

She hurried Chrissy to the car and loaded her into her safety seat. Once behind the wheel, Autumn looked in the rearview mirror to see if Greg followed them out of the store. She did not see him.

Autumn flicked on the air conditioner as she dialed Ray and told him about tomorrow's date with Greg. He told her not to worry. Thank goodness Ray was going with her to meet with Greg.

"It was so odd," said Autumn, "He was browsing in the cookbook section."

"Maybe he likes to cook."

"Or he intentionally followed us there."

A shiver went through her.

"We'll settle all of this tomorrow."

She hung up, Greg Manning weighing on her mind, and then checked her side mirror and looked back to ensure no cars were coming. She looked once more to double check. She signaled left as she carefully pulled out of the parking space. A car came shooting down the street in the opposite direction, the bend in the road making it look like it was coming straight at them, causing Autumn to suck in her breath and her heart to pound. Chrissy was on it, barking her sharp warning to take Autumn's attention away from the panic attack.

"Feel your feet on the floor," she said to herself, and then to Chrissy, "Thank you, sweetheart."

Chrissy grumbled and then made a guttural sound that seemed like she was scolding Autumn.

Autumn laughed and bent to kiss Chrissy's head.

"You're such a treasure."

With a deep breath, Autumn checked the mirrors and behind her once again, and then pulled out, making it onto the road this time. It was a short, uneventful drive to her psychiatrist's office. Autumn sighed with relief when they pulled into a parking spot in front of Doctor Wesley Harper's building.

Lifting Chrissy from her car seat, she gave her fur baby a loving squeeze and put her gently on the ground. Chrissy shook off and trotted up the steps to the entrance. She knew where she was. They had been there once a week and then once every two weeks for the last three months. Chrissy led the way to Doctor Wes's office door and waited for Autumn to open it. Her tail high and wagging, she greeted the receptionist.

"Who's that good girl?" the receptionist cooed while petting Chrissy's back.

Having been acknowledged, Chrissy went back to sit with Autumn. Doctor Wes came out a few minutes later and welcomed them in.

Autumn took off Chrissy's harness so she could freely interact with Doctor Wes.

"Hello there," he said and ruffled her hair.

She smiled and shook her hair back into place, then jumped onto the leather sofa and snuggled next to Autumn.

Dr. Wes took his usual seat across from the couch and opened his notebook.

"How are things?"

Autumn sighed and squeezed Chrissy against her.

"Lots of things have happened since we were last here. Ray and Chrissy have been great."

"I'm glad to hear you've been relying more on your support network."

"Me, too. I'm also trying to manage on my own as much as possible."

"What's been going on?"

"I had a partial panic attack on the way here. I was pulling away from the curb and a car came around the corner. It seemed like the car was coming right at us. Thankfully, Chrissy made short work of that. Because of her, it only lasted a minute or two."

Dr. Wes smiled as he made a note. Chrissy beat her tail against the cushion.

"That's excellent progress. Even if the anxiety bubbles up, it's best to catch it before it turns into a full-blown panic attack. Chrissy seems tuned into your signals."

"Yes she is!" Autumn praised Chrissy and kissed her head. Chrissy grunted in agreement.

Autumn thought a moment. "I've had far fewer panic attacks in the last two weeks than the two weeks prior. I've just realized that."

"Since the attacks are situational, could it be that you're driving less?"

"Yes. When I'm with Ray or my friend, Stephanie, they drive."

"And when you do drive, you always have Chrissy with you, correct?"

"Yes, and I use the trick of feeling my feet on the floor. That really helps."

"Good. If you're open to it, we can start a regimen of systematic desensitization at your next session. We'll use video and creative visualization to gradually expose you to anxiety-provoking driving scenarios and couple them with relaxation and positive thoughts. This method helps lessen your reaction when it happens in real time. How does that sound?"

"Let's try it. I'm so ready to take back control."

"Okay. What else has been going on?"

"I found out something shocking that changes my whole sense of who I am."

"Tell me about that."

Autumn hesitated, not wanting to say the words but unable to skirt the issue.

"My father lied to me."

"About what?"

"About who I am. I recently discovered that my lineage is with the Peabody family rather than the Clarkes."

Doctor Wes waited as Autumn took a deep breath.

"My great-grandmother, Daphne Adams Clarke, had an affair with Horatio Peabody. They were parents to my grandfather, Allen. My father knew but never told me that we are part of the Peabody clan."

"So you feel betrayed—"

"Yes! And deprived! I had an entire family I never knew. Now one of them is dead, and it's too late."

"Who died?"

"Oxnard Peabody. He seemed lonely, and we might have become friends. I was there the day he passed. No one, including his sister, Beatrice, seems to care."

"Your sense of self has shifted as a result of this knowledge."

"Absolutely. I always thought of myself as a Clarke. Now when I say my name, it feels like the lie gets repeated. Dad should have told me!"

"What if he had?"

Autumn thought about this.

"I could have asked questions. I would have had more time to acclimate to the idea. We should have talked about it and what it means to our family."

"Without the benefit of talking this through with your father, what have you learned through other sources?"

"That I inherited a fortune and the Peabody Mansion."

"What else?"

"That Dad was prohibited from sharing the information with me until it was time for me to inherit."

"Is it possible that he tried to protect you from gossip and ridicule? Your integration into the community may have been affected."

"I suppose so, but it will certainly be affected now. Between Beatrice's resentment of me and the town having suspected something was off, I have to face this alone."

Chrissy said, "grr" and looked at Autumn.

"Like Chrissy said, you're not alone. You have close ties with friends and neighbors. You have Ray, who stood beside you after finding out about your trauma when you thought he wouldn't. Have you told him about this?"

"Yes. He's been to the Peabody Mansion with me and is investigating Oxnard's death. It's likely murder, and Ray is worried that I may be in danger."

"His behavior speaks volumes. He is consistently protective and ultimately supportive. After you told him, did he give you the feeling that he wanted out of the relationship?"

"No."

"Did your friends want nothing to do with you because your great-grandparents had an illicit affair?"

"No."

"Have your core values changed as a result of discovering your true bloodline?"

"I guess not."

Doctor Wes paused to let it sink in.

"News like this understandably creates upheaval within the family unit and within the self. You've already shown people who you are as a person. Those closest to you don't seem to care about your windfall, unless they show happiness for you."

"They have."

"They likely don't put too much stock in your lineage as it pertains to your character, except that they might find it interesting from a historical perspective. Those who are not your allies won't support you either way. The gossips have probably been speculating for decades no differently than they are now, except that they've gotten confirmation of their suspicions."

"True."

"One thing I've learned is that nothing is revealed before its time. Not before we're ready. Having this information before now would have brought your self-identity into greater question than it does now. You had a chance to develop as an adult before dealing with the burden of your family history."

Autumn considered this. She looked into Doctor Wes's eyes and saw his care and wisdom. His words eased her pain. She nodded in agreement.

"How are you feeling now?"

"Better." Autumn took a deep breath and let it out.

"From what I can see, you're still the caring person you've always been. Your concern for Oxnard being lonely is extraordinary. You're not focused on the inheritance, but rather on the wellbeing of another human being."

"I still wish I'd had the chance to talk to Dad about this."

"He imparted his life philosophy onto you. That's your lineage and your birthright. Kindness, responsibility, and love are the values you inherited from him. Let them guide you in this situation."

Autumn nodded. What Doctor Wes was saying lifted her heart and moved the lump in her throat and stomach. She felt herself relax.

"All of that is true. Those are the criteria I'll use to make decisions in this matter as in all others, starting with making funeral arrangements for Oxnard."

⚞ 13 ⚟

"Mr. Thornburg, please. Autumn, uh, Clarke, calling."

The name she grew up with felt awkward. Saying it aloud took her off center.

"One moment."

"Hello, Ms. Clarke."

"Mr. Thornburg, have funeral arrangements been made for Oxnard?"

"I've made arrangements to cremate the body once the medical examiner is finished with it. The remains will reside in the family mausoleum at Forest Hills. By the way, as a relative, you also have a space reserved for you when the time comes."

Autumn's breath caught at the thought of being part of the Peabody clan for eternity. Her father chose his final resting place under a tree at Forest Hills. He and her mother purchased the plots years before they needed them.

"Has anyone considered doing a memorial service for him?"

"Nothing that's been brought to my attention. I could contact Beatrice if you'd like."

"Yes, please. If she hasn't planned anything, I will."

"Okay. Also, have you given any thought to legally changing your name to Peabody?"

Autumn was shocked at the suggestion.

"Not really."

"Well, you'd be within your legal rights to do so. I can take care of it for you if you'd like."

Changing her name would make the break from her identity with the Clarke family permanent. Options flew through her mind. Maybe a hyphenated name was the solution. Clarke-Peabody. Peabody-Clarke. Or maybe a middle name, would work: Autumn Clarke Peabody. Autumn Peabody Clarke. It all felt odd and confirmed that she was not ready to make a decision.

"Let me think about it. By the way, is there any sort of contract with Greg Manning for his work at the Peabody Mansion?"

"Nothing formal, why?"

"I'm evaluating his duties and whether or not to keep him on staff. Any thoughts on that?"

"Greg has been with the family since he graduated from high school. There's never been a formal contract. You're not obligated to keep him on."

"Did Oxnard trust him?"

"He didn't mention anything about trusting him or not. Do you have concerns about him?"

"He seems angry and sulks when he's around. It doesn't give me a good feeling."

"Would you like me to meet with him?"

"Maybe, but not yet. I'm bringing Detective Reed with me to meet with him tomorrow and go over his duties and daily routine."

"Okay. Also, the bank transfer is completed, so you have access to your inheritance."

"Thank you."

"I'll be in touch."

CR&O

It was almost dinnertime when Michael Thornburg called her back.

"Beatrice is not interested in arranging a memorial service for her brother."

"Does she mind if I do?"

"She indicated her displeasure at the suggestion, but there's really nothing she can do to stop you."

Autumn sighed. "She'll be angry either way, so I'll forge ahead. He deserves an appropriate send-off."

"Agreed. There is a separate fund to pay Oxnard's final expenses, so have the invoices sent to me for payment."

"I will. Thanks, Mr. Thornburg."

Autumn clicked off wondering how Beatrice lived without love and compassion in her life. She thought about possible locations for the ceremony and then realized that the Peabody Mansion was the perfect place. It was large enough for the likely crowd who wished to pay their respects to Oxnard and it was a family property. Her first call was to Lisa Coleman.

"Hi, Lisa!"

"Hey, Autumn. How are you doing?"

"Hanging in there. Listen, I'm putting together a memorial service for Oxnard Peabody at the Peabody Mansion a week from tomorrow from 1 pm to 5 pm and wondered if you're interested in providing refreshments."

"You are? Why you?"

Autumn forgot that most people did not know about her recent news.

"Well, uh, actually, turns out he was my cousin."

"No way!"

"Yes, my heritage comes as a surprise to me, as well. I'll tell you the whole story if you make me your special linguini with *fra diavolo* sauce."

Lisa chuckled. "To get that story, I'll go one better. You, Chrissy, Ray, and Ace come over to Dad's tomorrow night and I'll even throw in garlic bread. Mickey and Dad will be thrilled."

"Deal! And you're saying yes to providing refreshments for the service, right?"

"Yes. The challenge is not knowing how many people are attending, but I'll figure it out."

"We can do that at dinner tomorrow. Then you can give me a quote. This might be a great promotional opportunity for your restaurant, too, so make sure to put business cards on the serving tables."

"Great idea. See you tomorrow night around 6:30?"

"Yep."

Autumn hung up, thinking Oxnard would be okay with Lisa taking advantage of an opportunity. She dialed Ray next and told him about dinner. The man had a healthy appetite and loved Lisa's cooking, so he was in.

"Are you sure about having the memorial service at Peabody Mansion? It's your private space."

"It isn't like I live there right now. But there are things I'd like to safeguard from those looking for a souvenir."

"A few off-duty policemen moonlight as private security guards. I can ask if they're available a week from tomorrow."

"Perfect."

"I have some things I need to do tonight, but I'll see you bright and early tomorrow morning. Meeting with Greg should be interesting."

"No doubt about that."

It was the first night in weeks that she would not see Ray. Her frazzled nerves wanted to talk through all that was happening. Her next call was to Stephanie.

"Hey, Steph."

"Autumn! What's up?"

"Feel like having dinner tonight?"

"Sure. I'll bring some chilled Chardonnay. See you in a half hour."

Autumn felt eyes on her and turned to see Chrissy staring and licking her lips.

"Are you hungry, little girl?"

Chrissy smiled. Autumn filled Chrissy's crystal bowl with grain-free food to just below the rim. If she put in too much, Chrissy ate her fill and then walked away, leaving the rest. Her baby knew when she had had enough. A bowl of fresh, filtered water and a kiss on Chrissy's head, and she was all set to eat.

While Chrissy enjoyed each nugget, chewing several times before swallowing, Autumn threw together a salad. The mixed greens, avocado, tomato, hard-boiled egg, radish, and baked tuna steaks were perfect with the cold wine for a hot summer night. The doorbell rang just as Chrissy ate the last morsel.

Chrissy beat Autumn to the door, tail wagging furiously when she saw Stephanie. Stephanie bent down to rub her chest and belly.

"Hi, hi, hi sweetheart!" said Stephanie in rhythm with the rubbing.

"She certainly loves her Aunt Stephanie!"

Chrissy flipped over and trotted back to get a long drink of water. The sound of lapping accompanied them into the kitchen where wine glasses waited. Autumn removed the tuna from the oven, added a citrus dressing to the salad, filled two wide bowls with the mixture, and plopped the tuna on top.

"Grab the glasses, will you?"

Stephanie uncorked the wine and grabbed the glasses, then followed Autumn into the dining room where places were set with napkins and utensils. Chrissy came in, carrying a gourmet peanut butter dog cookie.

"Is that delicious?" Autumn asked her.

Chrissy settled next to Autumn's chair, cookie between her paws, teeth scraping as she worked the edge of the bone-shaped treat.

"She's been carrying that cookie around for a week. Likes to take her time."

"She's adorable," Stephanie said and sipped some wine. "Makes me think about adopting one myself."

Autumn was chewing, so she nodded agreement.

"But I'm not sure my schedule is right to have a dog."

"In the meantime, you can play with Chrissy anytime you want."

It was Stephanie's turn to nod with her mouth full.

"Thanks. This is so good, Autumn."

"So's the wine." Autumn took a sip.

"What's going on with the case? Any new developments?"

"We found thallium in the basement of the house. Ray took it to the lab. He's coming with me to meet with Greg Manning tomorrow and talk about his future working for me."

"And?"

"He gives me the creeps. I don't trust him."

Stephanie sipped more wine.

"I went to the bookstore to talk to Barbara McCarthy and ran into Greg in the cookbook aisle. What would he be doing in there? Following me?"

Stephanie gulped some wine. "He wasn't following you."

"How do you know?"

"I went in Attic Treasures last week and saw Greg wrapped around Barbara. They were joined at the lips."

Autumn choked on her food and took a drink to wash it down. She stared at Stephanie.

"Ray thinks Greg and Beatrice are an item. He caught Greg leaning over Beatrice like they were about to kiss."

Stephanie threw down her fork.

"Still interested in this clown?"

"No," Stephanie said with a pout.

Autumn laid her fork gently on the plate and reached out for Stephanie's hand.

"The right one will come along, someone worthy of you. We both know it's definitely not Greg. He's a womanizer, but also may be downright dangerous. What you saw adds to my worry about him. I'm not comfortable with him skulking around the property."

Stephanie nodded, gave a wan smile, and squeezed Autumn's hand.

"Good. Now let's finish dinner and the wine. I have something special for dessert."

Autumn knew it was not a good time to discuss her own issues or the leads she found. Stephanie required some loving attention, which Autumn and Chrissy gladly provided.

≈ 14 ≈

Ray and Ace picked them up at nine o'clock on Saturday morning to head over to the Peabody Mansion. Chrissy and Autumn gave Ray a kiss before settling into their car seats.

"Did you miss me last night?" Ray asked grinning.

"I had dinner with Stephanie."

"How is she?"

"Not great. She had her romantic sights on Greg Manning, but walked in on an intimate embrace with Barbara McCarthy over at the bookstore."

"That could explain what he was doing there in the cookbook section."

"I'm sure it has a lot to do with it. Do you think Barbara and Greg could be in on Oxnard's death?"

"She's not at the top of my suspect list."

"Barbara gave me a weird feeling when I hired her to look up the woman in the photo. She wasn't as friendly as usual, like she knew something she wasn't saying."

"You may have interrupted their tryst."

"That's true. Maybe she wanted to get back to Greg. Or maybe Greg told her I inherited the mansion and locked him out."

Ray nodded while he turned left onto Evergreen Road and pulled up to the mansion. Ray got out of the vehicle first and went to the other side to retrieve Autumn and the pups.

Greg leaned against the stone doorframe, arms crossed, muscles bulging, wearing jeans, a graphic T-shirt with the name of a local hardware store across the front, and a scowl.

"Good morning," said Autumn, getting her keys out to open the door.

Ray nodded in greeting.

Greg grunted in acknowledgment.

They entered the foyer and experienced a temperature drop of ten degrees from the outside heat. The phenomenon continued to amaze Autumn.

"Let's sit in the den," she said. The two- and four-legged members of the group followed her into the cozy room.

Ray caught Greg scanning the room, his gaze lingering when he looked near and then sat in the chair where Chrissy had found the diary. Autumn and Ray sat on the sofa. Ace and Chrissy found a sunny spot on the area rug.

Autumn began while Ray stayed vigilant of Greg's reaction to her questions.

"I understand you've worked here since high school."

"That's right."

"What are your duties as agreed to with Oxnard?"

"I take care of the inside and outside of this property and the outside of his residence."

"Jasper takes care of the inside of Oxnard's house, correct?

"Yes. And it's Beatrice's house now." Greg's fingers curled into his palms.

"Right. No one's seen Jasper since the festival."

"Including me." Ray noticed Greg's lip curl into a sneer.

"Has his disappearance added to your duties at Beatrice's house?"

"No. They'll stay the same."

"I plan to oversee the inside of the Peabody Mansion," said Autumn.

Greg crossed his arms and his legs.

Autumn continued, "You don't seem very happy with the new circumstances."

Greg's arms shot up and out then grabbed the arms of the chair and launched himself to his feet yelling. "Why would I be? You're disrupting my whole life. I had a good thing going here. Beatrice should have been the one to inherit this house."

Ray stood, positioning himself between Greg and Autumn. Ace got to his feet, bared his teeth, and growled. Chrissy followed suit, standing her ground while letting out sharp warning barks that lifted her front paws off the floor. Greg, wary of where this was going, looked at Ray and then Ace in turn.

"I don't have to take this crap. I quit!"

"That's fine with us. Leave all your keys and tools belonging to the mansion before you leave," commanded Ray. They had changed every lock on every door at the mansion, but asking Greg to relinquish his keys symbolized the official end of his time as caretaker.

Greg fished in his pocket and threw the keys onto the coffee table, and then stomped out of the room, giving Ace a wide berth.

They heard the heavy front door slam. Ray put his arm around Autumn. She took a deep breath, feeling safe in his arms.

"You okay?"

She unclenched her jaw and hugged him tight.

"Thank goodness you and Ace were here. I guess that didn't go well."

"On the contrary, I'd say it was the perfect end. You didn't have to fire him, and he's out of your hair."

"For now," said Autumn, burying her head into Ray's firm chest.

Chrissy let out a low *grrr*. Autumn released Ray and went over to her. She petted Ace's head and lifted Chrissy off the floor.

"You guys were awesome!"

Chrissy grunted and licked Autumn's cheek.

"Okay, help me figure out the flow for Oxnard's memorial service."

Autumn pulled out a notepad and wrote her list. First order of business was to get a cleaning crew. Second was security. She showed the list to Ray.

"I spoke to some of the off-duty officers last night. Three are available to help out."

Autumn crossed it off the list.

The large reception table in the foyer would hold prayer cards and flowers with a photo of Oxnard. Autumn wrote *order prayer cards* and *flowers* separately on her list.

"I love how organized you are," said Ray.

She smiled at him.

They walked into the kitchen, which seemed in good order. The stainless steel range, hood, and backsplash were commercial grade. The concrete countertops had an industrial feel.

"Lisa Coleman is making the refreshments. She needs to come see the kitchen." Autumn made another note.

In the expansive living room, they decided to put the urn, Oxnard's portrait, and a podium in front of the large arched window. Autumn made her notes.

"This place is amazing. Are you really thinking of moving in here?"

"I still don't know. I love it, but my parents' house holds a lot of memories for me."

"When I was in my treatment program, we were told to avoid things that brought back memories of the trauma. You had a great relationship with your parents, but it makes you sad to go into their bedroom."

Autumn pressed her lips together.

"If you stay in that house, at some point you might want to make it your own, redecorate, donate some of the stuff. Make the house ready to create new memories while keeping the love you had growing up."

Autumn went up on tiptoe and kissed him. He stroked her hair.

"I'll think about what you said."

"I just want you to be happy."

"We're going to need folding chairs in here for the service." She scratched it onto the notepad.

"And someone to preside over the ceremony."

"I don't know if Oxnard had any religious affiliation. I'll ask Mr. Thornburg."

They locked up and headed back to Autumn's house.

"You might think about an alarm system for the mansion. And it's not a bad idea to beef-up security at your house, too."

"Yeah, there are enough people mad at me to warrant that." She smiled.

Back at the house, Chrissy and Ace ran into the kitchen for water and then into the den to take apart the toy pile and pounce on anything with a squeaker. Autumn made iced tea and she and Ray settled onto the couch in the den watching the pups. Ace grabbed a stuffed dog with six squeakers in it and shook it vigorously. Not to be outdone, Chrissy grabbed her small piggy toy and mimicked Ace. When Autumn and Ray's laughter died down, they refocused their attention on the evidence.

"I want to show you these photo albums. They tell a grim story about Abigail and Horatio Peabody's life."

They paged through the photographs, with Autumn explaining her theory about the mystery woman and piecing it together with the information from the diary. They got to the end of the second photo album. Wedged between the pages was a lock of hair with the words Abigail Peabody, 1935.

"That was the year she disappeared," Autumn said. "Could you take it to the lab and match it to the skeleton's DNA?"

"Yes, and also compare it to Oxnard's DNA sample. We can also test for thallium sulfate. "

Autumn looked at the clock.

"Let's head over to the Colemans'. Chrissy, want to see Mickey?"

Chrissy's head snapped toward Autumn when she heard Mickey's name and then ran to the door. Autumn attached her harness and grabbed Chrissy's loaded to-go bag decorated with Shih tzus wearing diamond necklaces. It contained her travel bowls; a serving of food;

snacks, with some extra for Mickey; and filtered water. Ray picked the gift-wrapped red and white wine bottles off the counter, along with the thermal bag containing Ace's food and supplies. Ace waited at the door with Chrissy. Ray fastened the leash to his collar, and the group made their way down the street toward the Colemans' house.

"Do you think it's too soon to tell people about my heritage? I'm still getting used to it myself."

"What are you worried about?"

"That they'll see me differently than before, especially with the inheritance and all."

Ray nodded and wiped sweat from his brow.

"That's their problem. As far as I can tell, you haven't changed a bit, except for having a little more stress than usual."

Autumn pushed his shoulder. "Yeah, just a little more stress."

He smiled.

Everyone stopped when Chrissy squatted and Ace covered her mark with his own.

They heard Mickey barking in welcome as they walked up the path to the front door. Steve opened the door and got them in out of the heat. The air conditioning felt great. He led them into the kitchen where they put their bags down on the table and unhooked Chrissy and Ace.

"Hey guys," said Lisa from her place at the stove. She was stirring a pot.

"Something smells delicious! I'm starving," said Ray.

"I made a lot, so I'm glad you're hungry. How about opening the wine?"

Ray and Steve each grabbed a bottle and opened them, pouring glasses of red for Autumn and Steve and white for Ray and Lisa. They clinked glasses toasting friendship.

Autumn asked, "Can I help?"

"How about setting the table? Dad, can you show her where everything is?"

Steve and Autumn took everything into the dining room and set the places, while Ray set out bowls for Chrissy and Ace.

"Where are the pups?" asked Autumn.

"In the den where all of Mickey's toys are," said Steve.

"Then we'll wait to put out their food. Did Mickey eat already?"

"Not yet."

Lisa asked, "Ray, would you get the garlic bread from the oven?"

He put it in a basket and brought it out to the table. Lisa put the pasta and sauce in a large serving bowl and the meatballs in a separate dish. Grated cheese was already on the table. Ray brought the bottles of wine, while Autumn filled water glasses.

"All set. Let's eat!" said Lisa.

They took their seats. As Lisa pulled a precut hunk of garlic bread from the basket, she looked at Autumn.

"Well? Tell me about your cousin."

Autumn smiled and took a sip of wine.

"When Oxnard became ill, his attorney called me. They revealed that my father's grandmother Daphne had an affair with Horatio Peabody. She gave birth to my grandfather and named him Allen Clarke to avoid scandal. Although he was the product of Daphne and Horatio, my great-grandfather claimed him as his own."

She looked around the table. Ray was into his food. He had heard this story before. Steve chewed slowly, distracted by the news. Lisa's mouth hung open, garlic bread still in her hand. Autumn took a sip of wine.

"Go on," Lisa said, shaking herself from the shock.

"No one knew because it was a family secret. They designed the will to skip Beatrice upon Oxnard's death. I became next in line to inherit. My father never told me that I was in line to inherit the Peabody fortune along with the Peabody Mansion."

Lisa's food sat untouched in her plate. She took a gulp of wine.

"How did Beatrice react?" asked Lisa.

"Oxnard kept the secret from his sister. She's beyond angry at both Oxnard and me."

"I bet," said Steve, sticking a fork into a browned meatball and then spooning extra sauce on top.

"It's not like she's destitute. Oxnard left her his house and several million dollars," said Ray.

"What are you going to do with the mansion?" asked Lisa.

"The place is amazing. You'll get good exposure at the memorial service."

"Thanks for that, but I mean are you moving into the mansion?"

Autumn chewed a mouthful of pasta.

"This is really good, Lisa."

"Glad you like it. So?"

Autumn washed down the food with water.

"I'm not sure yet." She glanced at Ray, who was taking a second piece of garlic bread and two more meatballs.

"We'd miss having you down the street, but it's not that far."

"That's the thing. I'd miss you guys, too, and everyone else on the street. Living close isn't the same as walking by and seeing if Mickey is up for a walk."

"That's some place," said Steve.

"It sure is, but I grew up here. All the memories of my parents are here."

"The place is huge — too big for one person," said Ray. "The house you live in is beautiful and spacious with a fenced yard for Chrissy."

Autumn was disappointed to hear him say *'for one person'* when she was hoping to hear him suggest that he would eventually be a permanent part of her life. At the same time, she knew him well enough that he would rather discuss it privately before implying it publicly. Besides, they had only been dating for four months.

"True."

Toenails clicking on tile in the kitchen announced Chrissy, Mickey, and Ace. The loud lapping of water gave Autumn a break from the conversation as she went to serve them dinner. She returned to the table and forked some pasta into her mouth.

Steve brushed crumbs from his hands and washed down the garlic bread with water. "Whenever I walk into your house I think of your parents. It's like they are still there."

"Yes, it is. That's part of what I like about it and also what's hard about living there. But then I think that eventually I want to have a place that has my own mark on it."

"You could redecorate," said Ray. "I'm available for consultations." He smiled and refilled his wine glass.

"What do you know about decorating?" Autumn said, her surprise coming out in a chuckle.

"I know what I like," Ray said, winking at her.

She hoped he was thinking about their lives together and living at her house.

"Lots to think about," said Lisa, starting to collect the dishes. "Anyone for dessert? The chocolate lava cake will be up in a few minutes!"

Dessert was as good as, if not better than the main course. Chrissy pressed her head against Autumn's leg and whined. Autumn picked her up and gave her a squeeze and a kiss on the head.

"You're a tired little angel," said Autumn.

With many thanks and hugs, they left for home, Autumn carrying Chrissy and Ray holding the doggy totes and Ace's leash.

At Autumn's door, Ray said, "I'm going to head home before I get too comfortable."

Autumn nodded. "Text me when you get home." She looked up at him. "Were you serious about helping me redecorate?"

"Sure. Things are heading in the right direction with us. If we make things permanent, this house has everything we need." He kissed the top of her head.

"I'm glad to hear you say that." She squeezed his hand and petted Ace. "Be careful driving."

From the doorway, she watched him load Ace in the car, happy at the thought of the two of them making this house their own.

⚞ 15 ⚟

Barbara McCarthy huddled in the backroom of the bookstore with the photo Autumn had given her and historical records of Knollwood. Her lame attempt to hide the shock of seeing a picture of her great-aunt still fooled Autumn. The family rumors about Great-Aunt Ann and Horatio Peabody whispered their way through generations of McCarthys, but Ann's disappearance was never resolved.

Abigail Peabody's departure coincided with Ann McCarthy's, but both families worked hard to quiet the gossip. Barbara had her own suspicions and resented that Great-Aunt Ann was part of the household staff at the Peabody Mansion and likely one of Horatio Peabody' many lovers. Was Ann a willing participant or taken against her will by Horatio as so many housekeepers had been before her?

A part of her felt sorry for Abigail Peabody having to live with a philandering husband. She would never stand for it herself. What would she do if Greg cheated on her? Even with no commitment in marriage, Barbara still expected monogamy.

She wondered how Abigail had dealt with it. The photo she saw showed Abigail with thinning hair, a sign of illness and possibly of poisoning. Was she the victim of Horatio's wrath and a victim herself? Barbara debated how much to tell Autumn.

❦

All the workers arrived within thirty minutes of each other, creating chaos that required Autumn to point and direct them to their respective areas. The rental company set-up padded folding chairs and a podium, along with a large easel to hold a flattering photograph of Oxnard provided by the Peabody Foundation Board of Directors. Lisa Coleman managed her area to ensure the rental company placed food tables and bistro sets for optimum guest flow.

Earlier that day, the cleaning staff had scrubbed the entire first floor from top to bottom. The slate floor gleamed before the workers arrived. Now dulled with footprints, Autumn made a call to the cleaning service to request a touch-up tomorrow when everyone was finished their work.

Chrissy sat in the window seat of the living room, finding peace and safety on the sunlit cushion. Autumn peeked in every so often to check on her little princess. Chrissy looked up every time and wagged her tail. It was their unspoken signal that everything was okay. If she needed water, a snack, or to go out, Chrissy would find Autumn and let her know.

The funeral home placed Oxnard's obituary in the local and regional newspapers and online. Autumn anticipated a large crowd to honor her late cousin. The funeral-home staff would assist in crowd control and setting up the prayer cards, urn, and boxes of tissues.

Julie and Brad Hall, Stephanie Douglas, and Steve Coleman promised to come early and fill-in wherever help was required. Autumn knew their real intention was moral support, but they did not want to imply that she needed it. Her neighbors were so much like her parents in that regard, supportive but not smothering — always there cheering her on. Autumn saw her parents smiling down on her, knowing they left her in good hands.

Being around Lisa Coleman and watching her work brought the two closer. Her big-sister pride in Lisa's accomplishments made the desire to help her succeed even greater.

C880

Ray finished meeting with the officers who volunteered for memorial-service duty. He emphasized the need to stay vigilant and to ensure nobody went upstairs or in the basement, especially Greg Manning. He showed the officers Greg's driver's license photo and briefed them on Greg's temperament. Despite their recent hostile parting, Ray anticipated Greg's appearance at the event.

Ray's cell phone rang, indicating the lab calling.

"Detective Reed."

"Hi, Ray," said the lab tech. "I have news for you. The DNA results are in. The samples from Oxnard Peabody and the skeleton from the park are not a match. Neither is there a match between the hair sample and the skeleton. It's unlikely that the skeleton is Abigail Peabody."

Ray thanked him and disconnected the call. The assumption that the skeleton was Abigail Peabody was now off the table. Ace looked up at him as Ray leaned back in his chair contemplating his next move.

C880

The line of mourners stretched around the building to get into the memorial service. At Autumn's invitation, Beatrice reluctantly stood in the receiving line next to her. Autumn could feel the agitation and resentment rising like steam off Beatrice as she looked at the space she felt was hers. Not even the steady stream of mourners could dowse the heat. With every, "I'm sorry for your loss"; "he was a good man" followed by a handshake or a hug, Beatrice scowled.

Autumn focused on each person giving condolences to keep her sadness from spilling over. She figured that those who stayed cared for Oxnard and the ones who gave their sympathy and left were there to see the inside of Peabody Mansion. Some looked surprised to see her in the role of a family member but did not express it outright. Others looked around and found their way into the refreshment area tasting Lisa's offerings and then taking her card before leaving.

The word would spread that Autumn Clarke was a Peabody descendant. She imagined the gossips saying "I knew it" or "*The rumors were true*" and thinking of the most heinous version of how that came to be, but she could not worry about that right now. The opportunity for damage control was in delivering Oxnard's eulogy.

Stephanie sat in a chair just behind Autumn, playing with Chrissy to keep her occupied and out of harm's way. Some of the visitors noticed her and commented on how pretty she was or how cute her yellow bows looked.

Ace sat at attention next to Ray, who stood off to the side, their presence quelling any outburst from Beatrice.

Doctor Wesley Harper was next in line, his warm hands surrounding hers.

"How are you holding up?"

Autumn shrugged, tears welling up, the memory of her parents' funeral mixing with sadness for the loss of a cousin she would never get to know. Doctor Wes patted her hand. He radiated comfort and care.

"Thank you for coming."

He nodded and moved on toward the urn before taking his seat.

Autumn looked around the reception hall and saw Steve Coleman and Mickey; Julie and Brad Hall with their Yorkie, Teddy; and Maureen Roberts in a cluster. She caught their attention and they waved. Maureen threw her a kiss. Autumn smiled, grateful to be surrounded by those who loved and cared about her. There was no need for them to get in line. They had already paid their respects and were there as moral support.

The brief encounter bolstered Autumn for the next hundred guests moving slowly through the doorway. Between Beatrice's angry energy and the smell of cologne, cigarette smoke, and sweat, the task exhausted Autumn. She made eye contact with Ray. His hard, vigilant glare toward the crowd softened as he gave her a brief smile that lifted her heart.

Autumn saw Ray's glower return as his attention turned to the next mourner in line: Greg Manning. His light tan sport jacket, black T-shirt, and khakis stood out in the sea of black clothing. Ace stood. Autumn's body tensed. The hired security officers appeared in the area, watching Greg.

Greg moved past Ray without a glance and gave Ace a wide berth. His focus remained on Beatrice. He held her hands and hugged her. Autumn saw him whisper in her ear but could not hear what he said. Beatrice's expression softened for a moment before hardening once again. Greg ignored Autumn and took a seat at the back of the main room.

Autumn looked at Ray and sighed, releasing the stress brought on by Greg's presence.

A few more mourners came through whom Autumn did not know personally but recognized as Peabody Foundation board members. Her research into the Peabody interests detailed their biographies. The majority of the board members were in attendance and came through the line. Autumn noticed how stiff and standoffish Beatrice was with everyone except Greg.

Barbara McCarthy appeared, concern on her face. She shook Autumn's hand while gently holding her arm and gave her condolences.

"I'm so sorry for your loss. Oxnard is irreplaceable."

"Yes, thank you."

"When you get time to catch your breath, stop by the shop. I have the report for you."

"I will."

Barbara gave her sympathy to Beatrice without touching her. She saw Greg and rushed over to claim the chair next to him.

Autumn noticed Beatrice's lip curl and her hands ball into fists as Barbara flipped her hair, leaned in close, and put her hand on Greg's thigh. Greg whispered something into Barbara's ear, and then slid slightly away from her. As if Oxnard's murder did not stir enough drama on its own, a love triangle added spice to the mix.

Jade Fisher of Jade's Jewelry was a few guests away in line. The black, tight-fitting dress sported a high neckline to display a large, pearl collar encrusted with shining gemstones. Jade's hair and makeup made her look like she stepped out of the pages of a fashion magazine. If a contest were held, she would win Best Dressed for a Funeral.

Beatrice would come in last, and Autumn decided she fell somewhere in the middle.

"I'm so sorry to hear about Oxnard. The last time I saw him was at the festival. You never know when it will be the last time you'll see someone," said Jade, squeezing Autumn's hands too tight, her grip stronger than Autumn anticipated.

"Yes, his death is a loss to us and to the community," said Autumn.

Beatrice scoffed. Jade raised her eyebrows at her.

"Losing a brother must be hard. I can see you're overwrought," said Jade with a smirk.

She turned back to Autumn. "That necklace looks great with your outfit. Be well."

The necklace had belonged to Autumn's mother. It had pink freshwater pearls dripping from a gold chain. Her hand gently touched it.

Autumn watched Jade's hips sway as she glided down the center isle looking for a seat. Her assuredness sank when she spotted Barbara McCarthy cozied-up to Greg Manning. Regaining her composure, she found a seat next to a man enticed by her movement and glanced back at Greg. Autumn observed the latest bit of drama in an already murky sea of entanglements and shook her head. She saw that Beatrice also noticed with a clenched jaw.

Michael Thornburg, the Peabodys' attorney, appeared in front of them giving the usual condolences. Beatrice said nothing, and Autumn thanked him for coming. He went to find a seat in the crowded memorial area.

The line finally ended, with the memorial area at standing room only and stragglers milling around in the reception hall and the refreshment area.

Stephanie handed Chrissy to Autumn. Beatrice strode ahead of Autumn, giving Greg a sideways glare as she passed. When she turned her head, Autumn saw Beatrice's lower lip curl into a sneer at Barbara's hand on Greg's shoulder, her head leaning into his. Greg caught the evil look and cringed as though Beatrice had physically reprimanded him.

Stephanie elbowed Autumn, their silent signal for *see?* Autumn looked at her with a subtle nod. Up ahead, Beatrice stomped to her reserved seat in the front of the room. Ray, Ace, Stephanie, and Chrissy walked Autumn to the front and sat between Beatrice and her.

The room quieted as the minister took the podium. Autumn was glad that Michael Thornburg had told her about Oxnard's affiliation with the local Interfaith church. Besides, with most of the town here, the church's inclusive philosophy provided a relatable memorial service.

"I'm Reverend Brian Hopewell from the Knollwood Interfaith Church. We honor all spiritual paths, and all are welcome. We extend our deepest sympathy to the friends and family of Oxnard Peabody. Thank you for being here to honor this great philanthropist and humanitarian. The Peabody family has a long history as benefactors to the community of Knollwood. The many charities, organizations, and individuals he served will feel Oxnard's absence. His sister, Beatrice Peabody, and his cousin, Autumn Clarke, are left behind to mourn his loss."

A low mumble rippled through the crowd. Autumn shifted in her seat. Ray put his hand on her leg. Chrissy snuggled against her. Stephanie held her hand. Tears flowed down her cheeks in part for Oxnard Peabody's death, in part for the grief for her parents, and in part for the love and support she received from Ray, Stephanie, and Chrissy.

From somewhere far away, Autumn heard Reverend Hopewell introduce Beatrice to come up and say a few words. Beatrice stood up and smoothed the back of her black and tan cotton dress. Autumn realized that Beatrice and Greg were dressed to match.

CRBO

Beatrice made her way to the podium and pulled an index card from her pocket. Looking out over the crowd, she fancied herself the queen of all she surveyed — except, of course, she was not. The mansion belonged to Autumn. The thought took her eyes to where Autumn sat surrounded by her friends. Why did some people have everything and others, no matter how hard they tried, have nothing?

She spotted Greg sandwiched between the affectionate attentions of Barbara McCarthy and glares coming from Jade Fisher. If Beatrice and Jade teamed up, they might be able to melt Greg into the floor. The audience waited.

"My brother left this world unexpectedly. He didn't know that this year's Peabody Festival would be his last. None of us knows what fate has in store. All we can do is hope that things turn out the way we want them to. As I've recently discovered, that isn't always the case, but I will forge ahead. Oxnard left behind a legacy I plan to continue as head of the Peabody Foundation, as he would have wanted. Thank you."

Groans from the board members sitting nearby made her pause before taking her seat, arms crossed.

CB&O

The reverend introduced Autumn next. She handed Chrissy to Stephanie and took her place behind the podium. Public speaking was not her forte. Her place was behind a computer, not in front of a large group. She pulled out a typewritten sheet and looked out among the mourners, picking out those she knew. Seeing friendly faces gave her courage.

"For many years I knew of Oxnard Peabody, the local celebrity and philanthropist, but never knew the man himself, and I certainly never guessed that we were related. When I was called to his sickbed and discovered my true heritage, I was overjoyed to find another relative and saddened by his condition. I looked forward to getting to know both Oxnard and Beatrice and sharing many celebrations together. But he succumbed to his illness, and those plans went with him. I wish we had more time together.

"During those last hours, his caring nature shined through. He shared as much as he could, and I got the sense that he tried to do the right thing, the honorable thing, when faced with difficult decisions. He told me he was tired and ready to leave this world. The heavy burdens he carried in life lifted from him in death."

Autumn saw some pull out tissues and dab their eyes.

"We are here today honoring a man who gave without expecting anything in return. He loved this community and sought to better each life he touched. His hard work and sense of commitment were apparent in all he set his mind to. He even volunteered to be dunked at the festival, fully dressed, to raise funds for the Foundation."

Mild chuckles came from the crowd.

"My hope is that we can band together and continue to lift and support one another and our community in Oxnard's memory. I'm grateful for the chance to have been with him during his final hours and for all of your good wishes, prayers, and kindness during this difficult time. Thank you for being here to remember Oxnard Peabody and give him a proper farewell. He will be missed."

She went back to her seat, avoiding Beatrice's stare. Ray and Stephanie both patted her for a job well done.

Reverend Hopewell invited whoever wished to speak an opportunity to take the microphone. Autumn was pleased at how many volunteered to share stories of Oxnard's kindness. Some told

96

humorous stories, and others shared their admiration for his hard work and leadership. With every story, Beatrice sunk deeper into her chair.

The finale was Psalm 23, spoken reverently by Reverend Hopewell, followed by an invitation to enjoy refreshments in the study.

Beatrice stormed off, conspicuously alone, while groups of people came up to Autumn, congratulating her on the eulogy and for being part of the Peabody clan. They accepted her as a Peabody, and she was getting used to being one.

CŊŊ

Beatrice made it to her car without speaking to a soul — not that anyone tried to engage her. They flocked to Autumn, who was not as much of a Peabody as she herself was. It irked her to share the spotlight and her heritage. Autumn knew nothing of what it meant to be a Peabody. Beatrice spoke her mind in front of Knollwood's residents and expected them to embrace her as their new leader in Oxnard's place. Instead, they pushed her aside in favor of the Clarke woman.

She saw Jade Fisher stepping across the asphalt parking area over to her ice blue Mercedes like a model strutting down a runway. Owning the exclusive shop for high-end jewelry designers must pay well for her to afford a car like that. But rumors existed that Jade's money came from some unknown and possibly shady source. With or without the money, some people were born stylish. Beatrice did not have that gift and looked dumpy regardless of her efforts.

Beatrice's thoughts turned to Greg and what a slime he proved to be. He did not engage Barbara McCarthy but seemed to enjoy the attention. Jade Fisher had a lot of nerve to be angry about Greg sitting with Barbara. She was nothing to him. If they knew that Greg Manning belonged to Beatrice, neither would dare make a play for him. The power Beatrice wielded trumped their beauty and style hands down.

A knock on her window startled her from her thoughts. Greg opened the door.

"What are you doing?"

"Getting away from watching you get pawed by another woman."

"Come on. She's nothing."

"She seemed pretty comfortable being close to you."

"Bea, you're the only one I want." He squeezed her upper arm and left his hand there. "You know we can't let people know we're

97

together. It's better if they think I'm with someone other than you. Barbara is just a decoy."

She liked it when he called her by the affectionate name Bea. Her father had called her that. Mistrust returned, and she pulled her arm away from his touch.

"I'm not in the mood for games."

"Okay, I'll be honest with you. Barbara told me that Autumn asked her to research Peabody's financial activities to see if she could get you off the board. I was trying to convince her not to do it."

"And did she have second thoughts?"

"It's hard to tell. I'll check up on her later."

"Just stay away from her."

Greg held his hands up in surrender. "Whatever you want."

"I'm going home."

"Which one?"

"My house. I don't want to be around Oxnard's things right now."

"Should I meet you there?" Greg gave her his most enticing smile. Beatrice looked at him. She did not trust him, but he was still useful. "Come for dinner around seven."

⋆⋆⋆

Barbara McCarthy walked to her car and spotted Greg talking to Beatrice. She figured he was giving final condolences for both the loss of her brother and for delivering that dreadful eulogy.

Barbara got in her car and headed to Attic Treasures with Greg on her mind. He said he might stop by later, but did not commit to a time or even to showing up. That was just like Greg. He hated being pinned down to a schedule. She wondered if he felt the same way about relationships. When she pushed him, his anger terrified her. Why was she wasting her time with him? Maybe it was time to try online dating.

She parked behind the building and let herself in through the back door. She flicked on the light switches on her way to the front door and flipped the sign to say *open*. With most of Knollwood at Oxnard's memorial service, she might get dribs and drabs of customers this afternoon. No matter, she had work to do.

The research folder for Autumn Clarke was on top of the pile of other jobs. Many of the cases involved family trees, which genealogy software programs made easy. Autumn's inquiry was unique in that it affected Barbara's family, too, because of her great-aunt being a housemaid for the Peabody family. That is what they were back then — more servant than independent contractor as they are today. Her mother told her stories about Great-Aunt Ann and the Peabody Mansion.

Ann, along with the rest of the town, felt sorry for Abigail, knowing about Horatio Peabody's philandering ways. For Ann especially, Horatio's disregard for his wife bothered her, as she was one of his conquests. As a servant, she had no choice but to comply with his wishes. Over time, Ann grew to love his attention and vie for status as his most desired affair. She could never be his wife; he already had one, and Horatio did not intend to get a divorce. Abigail had the right pedigree, which Ann did not, and Abigail made him look good in public.

When Abigail's hair began falling out, the town's rumor mill went wild. Suspected of being Horatio's latest conquest, fingers pointed at Ann. The gossips reasoned that she meant to do away with the wife who stood in her way, possibly with Horatio's blessing. Could she be serving tainted food to Abigail? As the whispers grew, Ann withdrew from public view and stopped contacting her friends and family, They never heard from her again.

Abigail's disappearance clinched the rumor, and a pall fell over the town of Knollwood.

Now Autumn wanted to know about Great-Aunt Ann from the photo. With Autumn's new status as a Peabody, she had a right to know.

Barbara finished writing the report, complete with her own family ties, and put it in a large manila envelope addressed to Autumn.

Her thoughts returned to Greg. He recently asked her to research Beatrice Peabody's background and dig up any dirt she could find. His primary interest was in her finances. The request had a sinister undertone. From cases she saw on the news, dark intentions went along with something like this, and she wanted no part of it.

Wanting to strike a balance between keeping Greg happy and staying away from whatever he had in mind, she suggested he do an online search using a background check company. Barbara punctuated her lack of experience in this type of research, saying that she was a town historian, not a private investigator. Greg insisted that he wanted it done or he would tell Beatrice that it was Barbara's idea, but Barbara refused.

She did not want him to get in trouble, which prevented her from sharing the burden of it with anyone else, including the local police. Besides, he had not done anything illegal as far as she knew, so all she could report was a request for information.

Since then, he did not stop by as often, so when she saw him at the memorial service, she took the opportunity to feel him out and give him some attention. He withdrew from her several times when she whispered in his ear and did not answer when she asked when they could be together again. Thinking about it, she decided to keep her distance from Greg Manning. He was more trouble than he was worth.

Barbara thought about Autumn's heartfelt eulogy. She wanted someone with a big heart to remember her fondly and say kind words about her at her own funeral. Right now, that desire had no chance of coming true.

The bell on the front door tinkled. She went to see if Greg decided she was worth his time.

03&80

Clean up was in full swing at the Peabody Mansion. Stephanie was in the corner grinning and chatting away with Adam Miller, one of the off-duty police officers. At least Stephanie's attention had shifted away from Greg.

Lisa packed the few remaining food items in to-go containers. Steve helped her load the serving platters and utensils in snug sleeves and arrange them in boxes. Autumn walked up and hugged Lisa.

"Thanks for the great job today, Lisa."

"People enjoyed the refreshments, and I have no business cards left!"

"That's what we wanted. Besides, I wouldn't trust anyone else with such an important day."

Lisa beamed.

"You did a wonderful job with the eulogy," said Steve.

"Thanks. It was all true."

Ray came through the front door with Chrissy, Ace, and Mickey leading the way. Chrissy tugged at the leash trying to get to Autumn. He removed her harness, and Chrissy bounded over to Autumn's waiting arms. Mickey was next, trotting over to Steve. Ace maintained his usual majestic stance and stayed next to Ray.

Autumn waved them over and pulled Ray into the study.

"The officer Stephanie is talking to. What do you think of him?"

"He's a good guy and is currently single."

"That may not be the case for long."

They entered the reception area, watching the two standing closer than they were only minutes ago.

"Stephanie, we're almost ready to leave," called Autumn.

Stephanie and the officer came over.

"Adam said my place is on the way, so he offered to take me home."

Lisa came up with a bag loaded with takeout containers.

"Here's a snack for the two of you. Desserts and finger sandwiches."

Adam's eyes lit up.

"Thank you. We could stop at the park on the way and have a picnic."

"Great idea," Stephanie said through the biggest smile Autumn had seen on her face in years.

They waved goodbye and closed the door against the humid day. Autumn suspected the heat would not bother them. The two of them were in a comfortable bubble, impervious to the outside world.

After helping Lisa and Steve pack the car, Ray, Autumn, and the pups went into the study and Ray and Autumn moved the sofa back into place before sitting down. Autumn kicked off her shoes and leaned against Ray. He put his arm around her. Chrissy jumped up and snuggled against her. She sighed, letting out the tension of the day. Ace cozied on the rug beneath them.

"What did you think of that drama going on between Greg, Beatrice, Barbara McCarthy, and Jade Fisher? I don't understand the attraction to Greg Manning. What do women see in him? He's creepy," said Autumn.

"Guys like him target lonely women and make them feel special. He's a classic manipulator and likely more than that. I'm waiting for him to make a wrong move."

"I'm happy that Stephanie made a better choice."

"I like Adam. We could go on double dates."

Autumn looked around the study with its heavy bookcases and carved fireplace mantel.

"I like this room. It's large but still cozy. Could you see uh, mmm, me living here?"

She almost said *us*.

Ray held her close.

"This place doesn't seem like it's meant for a family. I told you, your house is perfect for us."

She looked into his eyes. He nodded. She smiled.

"Hey, I just realized that Jasper Wiggins was absent from the crowd. For as long as he worked for Oxnard, you'd think he would pay his respects," said Autumn.

"Unless he's the reason Oxnard is dead."

They sat for a time, each absorbed in their own thoughts. When they opened the front door, the leaves dripped and the sun beamed through remaining clouds. The air was cooler, the work of an afternoon thunderstorm rolling through. The thick walls of the mansion insulated them from the noise, and Chrissy slept straight through it.

≈ 16 ≈

A peaceful Sunday gave Autumn a chance to unwind. Ray and Ace came over early for breakfast and they enjoyed a lazy day snacking and watching movies. They napped intermittently on the couch, with Chrissy mostly on them and Ace on the floor.

Now Autumn was ready to meet with Barbara on Monday and face whatever Barbara discovered about the mystery woman in the photo.

She found a parking spot in front of Attic Treasures. The sign on the door said *closed*, but the lights were on. Barbara was a stickler about time. She opened promptly at 10 a.m. each day, and it was 10:30 a.m. now. Maybe she forgot to turn the sign. Autumn tried the door.

The bell jingled as Autumn and Chrissy crept into the shop. Dim lighting cast eerie shadows across the stacks, the books abandoned.

"Barbara?" Autumn called into the dense quiet.

No answer. Maybe she had run across the street for coffee. They walked farther into the shop and past the desk.

"Barbara?"

Nothing. Chrissy barked once, making Autumn jump. She did the same thing at Mickey's house when Steve took too long to answer the door.

They made their way to the rear seating area where Barbara and Autumn had discussed the research project. Chrissy made a low growl. Autumn gasped when she saw Barbara lying motionless on the floor amidst a paper plate, plastic fork, mixed green salad, and what looked like jicama or parsnips drizzled with a yellowish dressing. Barbara had fallen on her side, and Autumn could see that there was no movement of her chest. Barbara's color was closer to white than her usual pinkish skin tone.

Chrissy sniffed Barbara's neck. Autumn pulled her away. She did not want Chrissy to disturb the scene or to inhale or ingest anything harmful. There was no telling what happened to Barbara, so it was best to be cautious. Autumn also worried about Chrissy having a triggering experience around a dead body. The skeleton was one thing; this body was more like when her daddy passed away. Chrissy was fine with all of it. Autumn wondered if she was growing accustomed to dead bodies or if her confidence resulted from the security Autumn provided. She hoped it was the latter.

She hit Ray on speed dial.

"Hey, honey."

"Ray, please come to Attic Treasures right away. We just found Barbara lying on the floor."

She could not bring herself to say *dead*.

Within fifteen minutes, the police and ambulance arrived. Everything in Knollwood was close by, and with normal traffic, anyone get anywhere in town lickety-split. Autumn and Chrissy waited outside on the bench, sweating in the August heat. Ray and Ace walked over.

"Are you all right?" Ray asked putting his hand on her shoulder. Chrissy grumbled and he petted her head.

Ace nuzzled Chrissy and sat on the ground beside her.

"For the most part."

She told him everything, leading up to finding Barbara. Ray wrote it all down.

"Everything is as we found it. We didn't touch anything, except Chrissy sniffed the body."

"That shouldn't hurt any evidence. Do you want someone to drive you home? I'll call you when we finish up here."

"I need to walk around. Window-shopping might be a good distraction."

"Okay," he squeezed her hand and went into the shop.

Autumn and Chrissy crossed the street, walked past a tailor shop, browsed in the clothing boutique, and then went into Jade's Jewelry. Chrissy sniffed the air as they walked into the shop. Jade was at the counter unpacking new deliveries, the sunlight making the necklaces, earrings, and bracelets sparkle. Jade looked up.

"It's Autumn and the Princess of Knollwood!"

Chrissy wagged her tail.

"What can I help you with today?" Jade grinned, now holding up new items from the boxes, especially the larger, more expensive pieces.

Everyone knew about Autumn's inheritance at this point. She got the sense that Jade planned to help her spend it.

"Just browsing."

"What's all the ruckus across the street?"

Autumn sighed. "We found Barbara on the floor of her shop. I called the police."

"My goodness! Is everything okay?"

"She wasn't moving. I don't want to jump to conclusions," even though Autumn was sure she was dead.

"So you called that handsome boyfriend of yours. I wouldn't mind stealing him away."

Autumn gave a weak smile. Jade posed no threat to her relationship with Ray. Besides, high-maintenance women were not Ray's type.

"Have you seen Barbara since the funeral?" Autumn picked through a box of earrings that were on sale.

"Can't say that I have. Maybe Greg knows. They looked pretty cozy at the memorial service."

"I saw you looking at them."

"Public displays of affection have no place at a memorial service."

"I guess not." Autumn held up a pair of moonstone drop earrings bound in sterling silver. "How much are these? There's no tag."

"They're on sale. Fifty-five dollars. There's also a pendant that goes with them." Jade held up the necklace showing the iridescence of the five moonstones dangling from the chain.

"Beautiful! Okay, I'll take that, too."

"Nothing for the little princess?"

Autumn looked down at Chrissy. She wagged her tail and made a *mrroww* sound.

Jade fished behind the counter.

"How about this white leather collar embedded with turquoise?"

"I didn't know you carried pet items."

"I bought a box of assorted pet jewelry after the fair. Lots of people had dogs with them."

Autumn took it and wrapped it around Chrissy's neck. It was pretty and light, but Chrissy's hair swept over it, covering the design. Autumn handed it back.

"Any new barrettes we could look at?"

Jade pulled out jeweled clips shaped like flowers. Autumn pinned them into Chrissy's hair.

"Perfect."

Jade smiled as Autumn pulled out her credit card. She surprised herself for spending this much money. She did not want to become a spendthrift regardless of her wealth. The small bag fit inside her purse.

"Thanks, Jade."

"I appreciate your business. You and the princess take care."

CঙৠO

105

Jade hung the newly unpacked necklaces on black displays. Autumn had seen her giving Greg the evil eye at the memorial service. Not good. She had a reputation to uphold as a desirable woman who could get any man she wanted. Barbara pawing at Greg took his attention away from her.

She draped bracelets across the black bar of the display stand. She sparkled brighter than the jewelry she carried. People noticed her. Greg usually noticed her. She tried taking advantage of his last visit to her shop, dragging him into the storeroom to make lasting memories, only to be pushed away after a brief interlude.

Barbara had to be the reason. She turned on the radio and sang to a love-done-me-wrong song.

Cℰℬↄↄ

Autumn walked back toward the bookshop. The ambulance had gone and some of the police vehicles remained. She spotted Ray's unmarked SUV. He waved her over.

Ace went up to Chrissy, and they sniffed each other, nose to nose.

Ray pointed to the shopping bag.

"Anything good?"

"A necklace and earrings for me and hair ornaments for Chrissy."

"I'll make dinner reservations so you both can show them off."

"Nothing too fancy."

Ray went to his vehicle and reached through the passenger-side window.

"This was in Barbara's outgoing mail bin. Her postage meter dated it for Saturday, so she intended to mail it that day since metered mail has to go out on the date of the label."

"The Post Office was closed after 1 p.m."

"She probably planned to put it in a mailbox."

"If we assume she came to the shop right after the funeral, it wouldn't have been later than 2 p.m. Add time to write or finish the report and stamp the envelope puts it around 4 p.m."

"The report may have already been written and she just needed to address the envelope and put a stamp on it."

Autumn nodded and took the envelope.

"Either way, it sounds likely that she's been here since Saturday."

"The timeframe fits according to the medical examiner."

"With the sign saying *closed*, a customer probably wouldn't try the door. Otherwise, she would have been found sooner."

"Right. Barbara either forgot to flip the sign to open—"

"Not likely," Autumn interjected. She was a stickler about making sure people knew she was open for business."

"—Or someone had to flip the sign to *closed*."

Autumn shivered at the thought of Barbara being murdered.

"I asked Jade Fisher when she saw Barbara last. She said at the memorial service and thought Greg might have more information."

Ray made a note.

"He seems to be in the middle of everything. I'll talk to him."

"Maybe you should add Beatrice to the list. She didn't seem too happy seeing Barbara with Greg. Jealousy is a motive, isn't it?"

"One of the oldest. I saw her giving Greg and Barbara the evil eye."

Autumn opened the envelope and pulled out the report.

"I can't wait to find out who the mystery woman in the photo is. I'll read it when I get home."

"I'll be over after work and you can update me, right Ace?"

Ace let out one loud, deep woof and nuzzled Chrissy before walking away with Ray.

☙

Autumn took Main Street and headed home in her usual, careful fashion. A gunmetal gray car came speeding around the bend and swerved toward her before moving back into its own lane. Autumn screamed and pulled over, panting. Chrissy let out short, sharp barks, forcing Autumn's attention onto her. Her breathing evened out as she petted Chrissy's head.

Her head cleared after a few minutes. Autumn put her hand on her chest, shocked at how quickly she recovered from the incident. She ruffled Chrissy's hair.

"What a good girl!"

Chrissy wagged her tail.

Then another realization struck: Beatrice was the driver of the vehicle. Autumn trembled, appalled that Beatrice would pull a dangerous stunt like that. How dare Beatrice try to push her into a panic attack? She probably got the idea from the news article in the local paper about the car accident that had killed her parents and how Autumn struggled with PTSD. Something snapped inside of her and all at once, her fear dissolved. She gripped the wheel and felt her feet on the floor this time to dispel the fury at Beatrice intentionally pushing the panic button. She refused to be a victim any longer.

With a deep breath, she put her left-turn signal on and pulled onto the road, thinking of ways to put Beatrice in her place once and for all.

Safe in the garage, she lifted Chrissy from her car seat and went into the house. She opened the sliding door to the yard, but Chrissy's excursion outside was short-lived, the heat being too oppressive to play. She ran over to her water bowl, lapped half of its contents, disappeared into the den, and then joined Autumn in the living room carrying her rawhide-alternative chewy stick. She settled onto the floor to gnaw at the treat. Autumn was happy to have finally found this type of chew made in the United States. Reading labels on dog food and treats was now a habit in the way she read the packaging of her own food.

The report was five pages of easy reading. No wonder Barbara had acted strangely at their first meeting. Having a stake in this story, she must have resented all Peabodys and blamed them for her great-aunt's abuse. The timing of Ann McCarthy's disappearance was oddly close to Abigail's. Did Horatio Peabody kill them both, or did the women decide they had had enough abuse and leave separately or maybe even together? Then the light bulb went off: could Ann McCarthy be the corpse found at the Peabody Festival?

She phoned Ray to let him know her theory, but the call went to voicemail. She told him what was in the report and suggested he have the medical examiner match a DNA sample from Barbara McCarthy to the skeleton. She clicked off with a *see you later*.

Autumn watched Chrissy stretched out on the floor holding her chew between her fluffy white paws. Autumn felt her heart open with love and gratitude for this little fuzz ball who had moved her past the worst part of her trauma; Autumn had done the same for her. A sense of contentment filled the room. Autumn looked at the comfortable surroundings. She could not imagine relinquishing her window seat to a new owner or having someone else cooking in her mother's kitchen.

She walked toward her parents' room and paused outside the door. With a deep breath, she turned the knob and stepped in. For the first time since their passing eight months ago, the air lacked their essence. She propped the door open. Chrissy sat at the doorway. Autumn had trained her not to go into this room. Now Autumn encouraged her to follow. She cautiously stepped across the threshold and looked around.

"It's okay, sweetheart."

Chrissy took a few more steps and sat.

Autumn opened her mother's walk-in closet. It had started smelling a bit musty. She moved the clothes around and pulled out one of her mother's favorite tops. Her mother had been stylish but her clothes were not Autumn's taste. She put it back and perused her shoes and purses. They no longer held her mother's energy. It was time to call the local veterans' association and make a clothing donation.

She went to her father's wide, organized closet and saw some shirts that might look good on Ray. She chose those items, bagging them for the dry cleaner. Ray could decide if he wanted anything before she donated her father's possessions.

The drawers were next, filled with undergarments, socks, sweaters, and knit tops that were more her style. She would keep many of the pieces, throw away the undergarments, and donate the rest. A sigh rattled from deep within her. Letting go was hard, but it was a step toward creating a new life. By accepting their deaths, she could build the happiness her parents wanted for her.

She ran her finger through the dust covering the dresser. She did not enter this room very often due to her emotional response to it.

Chrissy joined her in the middle of the spacious master suite. She sniffed the floor and explored the furniture and bedding.

Bottles of Chanel and Burberry sat on her mother's mirrored tray, never to be used again. It was a shame to throw them away. Autumn did not wear perfume. Maybe the real estate agent, Maureen Roberts, would like to have them.

Being able to part with her parents' possessions made it clear that she held them in her heart, carrying them with her always. She no longer needed their stuff.

Grabbing trash bags from the kitchen pantry, she started transforming the room from her parents' domain to her own, thinking about paint colors and furniture options. She might even renovate the en suite bathroom. It felt good to stop tormenting herself.

She opened one of her father's drawers and discovered collared knits in a variety of colors. She remembered he wore them to play golf. She took them out one at a time, assessing each to see which ones to set aside for Ray. Between a turquoise shirt emblazoned with a golf-course logo and a striped burnt-orange shirt was a sealed envelope with her name written in her father's hand.

Her heart leapt, and the excitement of having one last communication from Dad buzzed through her. She ran into the kitchen for a letter opener and slit the envelope open cleanly. Her hands trembled as she slid the letter from the envelope and slowly unfolded it as she walked back to the master bedroom. She sat on the bed, and Chrissy jumped up to join her.

Dearest Autumn,

If you're reading this, I must be gone. There are so many things I was prohibited from telling you about our family. We are of Peabody blood and, once your cousin, Oxnard Peabody, dies, you will be a very rich woman. Use the money and power wisely. I have prepared you for this all of your life. Do what makes you feel good inside. Live your life on your own terms, not in the shadow of the past.

I can hear you wanting to ask me a thousand questions like you always do. Within our family history lies deception and poor behavior, but that is not your legacy. Love is your heritage. Take it and shower it upon others. You have always been wealthy with affection and joy. Let all you do come from a place of love, and know that your mother and I are with you always.

Eternally yours, Dad

She heard his voice as she read. Autumn wished the letter was longer, but it told her what she needed to hear. Her father knew how she would react to the news of her family lineage and made it clear that her nature came from the love she grew up with and continued to receive from those around her. She realized that the love she gave to those around her marked who she was more than any bloodline.

She reached for Chrissy and hugged her tight. Autumn was creating a lineage of love with Chrissy, Ray, Ace, and all of her friends. Through compassion and care, she would set right the wrongs of the past.

She carefully refolded the letter, put it back in the envelope, and stored it upstairs in her current bedroom in a box with her most treasured memories. She planned to talk to Dr. Wes about it, but otherwise she would keep it just between her and her father.

"I've made a decision," Autumn said as she unpacked the groceries.

"Don't keep me in suspense," said Ray, as he tossed the ball to Ace and Chrissy.

The pups had a clear run from the kitchen table into the living room. Better they play in the air conditioning than the hot, humid yard.

"I'm keeping this house and renovating the master bedroom." She kept her eye on him to see his reaction and saw his broad smile.

"Excellent! I think we'll all be happier here."

She raised her eyebrows. Ray stammered.

"Well, you know, we spend a lot of time here and it's comfortable. That other place feels cold, and the ceilings are too high."

She smiled.

"Part of staying here means clearing out my parents' clothes. Dad has some great stuff I'd like you to look at."

Ray stopped throwing the ball.

"Are you sure? I mean, it might be hard seeing me wear his clothes."

Autumn pressed her lips together. He knew her better than she realized.

"I thought of that. I think it would remind me of him in a good way. He would have liked you."

Chrissy and Ace barked for another toss.

"That's it for now. Go play in the den."

They stared at him the way they begged for treats.

"Go on," Ray said. "What's in Chrissy's toy pile?"

The two furry friends ran into the den. They recognized the words *toy pile*.

"Let's go look and see if you like anything. The charity truck is coming to pick everything up day after tomorrow."

"What time are Adam and Stephanie coming for dinner?"

"We have a few hours. Plenty of time to try on some clothes and make dinner."

Ray got up from the table.

"Why the sudden change of heart?"

"After Beatrice pretended to run me off the road, my usual panic attack started, Chrissy pulled me out of it, and then I got mad. I'm tired of feeling helpless. Besides, my dad's advice popped in. He always said don't be a victim."

Ray nodded.

"Anger is a good way to overcome fear. I experienced that when my PTSD lessened. The frustration of feeling out of control helped me manage the symptoms. That, plus therapy."

"Yeah, Dr. Wes is great. Even though I'm off the meds, my visits with him keep me balanced." Autumn paused. "A big part of my recovery has to do with Chrissy—and with you."

Ray got up and hugged her.

"Thanks for making me feel safe."

Wrapped in his strong arms, nothing could harm her. He pushed her away to look at her face.

"You make me feel that way, too."

His kiss was warm and loving.

"I'll always miss my parents, but I'm finding ways to remember the good times instead of the accident. Let's see how I react to you wearing Dad's clothes, and we'll go from there."

Ray put his arm around her as they walked to the master bedroom.

Her mother's clothes filled ten large boxes, one on top of the other in the corner. Ray peered into the large closet, its doors open and the space empty. Autumn slid her father's closet door aside. Select pieces remained on hangers. Sweaters, shirts, and ties hung neatly in dry cleaner plastic, the rest packed into another seven boxes.

"These are nice!" Ray said.

He perused the cardigans, dress and casual shirts, ties, and collared knits.

"I'd never be able to afford these on my salary. Thank you!"

"Try on this cable knit cardigan."

It fit him perfectly, and the burgundy color suited him. Ray looked in the mirror.

"I like it. It's not something I'm used to wearing, but it looks good."

Autumn gazed at him, her father's image coming forward. George Clarke liked wearing this sweater to brunch or on chilly weekend days. As his image faded, Ray came into view and gave the garment a completely new energy.

"It does look good." Autumn sniffed back some tears.

"You okay?" Ray slid off the sweater.

"Absolutely. This phase of the process is hard, but necessary. I like seeing you in it."

He chose some other sweaters, pullovers, shirts, and knits. Autumn put them in a small suitcase, roomy enough to fit all of the clothes. She remembered that when George and Stella Clarke went on weekend getaways, they took that bag with them.

Ray lugged it out to the car, along with a smaller tote filled with ties.

Autumn hummed to herself as she cooked for their guests.

Ray hugged her around the waist from behind.

"Can I help?"

"Sure. How about making the salad and feeding the pups?"

On cue, the two four legged friends rushed into the kitchen to lap water and ask for dinner.

"I'm on it!"

⋖⋗

Stephanie and Adam were right on time and brought wine to go with the antipasto platter.

"You have a lovely home, Autumn," Adam said between bites of Italian bread topped with provolone cheese.

"Thank you. I plan to stay here."

"You decided!" said Stephanie, her excitement bringing a puzzled look to Adam's face. She turned to him and explained. "As the new owner of the Peabody Mansion, Autumn could move in there or stay here. This is her family's home."

The thought that she now considered both buildings her families' homes crossed her mind.

Adam said, "I like this better. The mansion doesn't feel like a residence. It's more like a hotel." He took a sip of wine. "Don't get me wrong. The other place is amazing, but not to live there."

"How was your picnic? Did you get caught in the storm?" asked Ray.

"We decided to go for coffee and dessert instead, so we were indoors when the sky opened up," said Stephanie.

She was more at ease than Autumn had ever seen her. Stephanie's behavior was usually erratic around a new boyfriend. Officer Adam Miller had a calming effect on her.

"Thanks for hiring me as security for the memorial service. If you hadn't, I never would have met Stephanie."

Stephanie blushed.

"You served as an imposing figure to the guests. Potential drama was everywhere," Autumn said, covering a cracker with tapenade.

"You're not kidding," said Adam. "That woman standing next to you in the receiving line looked like she hated everyone in the room."

"That's close to the truth," said Autumn.

"Her brother died, and she showed no grief. I don't get it. I'm not a crier, but when my cousin passed away, I wept at her funeral," Adam said, taking another piece of cheese.

"She has a lot of anger. From the first time I met her, she disliked me. I guess I can understand, since I inherited the house she always wanted."

Ray cautioned her, "Please stay away from her unless absolutely necessary. So far, she's only threatened you, including with the car incident. One day she may follow through and really hurt you."

Adam nodded to the rhythm of his chewing.

Stephanie chimed in. "Remember, I was there that first time. Listen to them."

"I want to believe she's redeemable. Maybe she had a rough childhood. I don't know. I'll keep it under advisement. In the meantime, let's eat!"

A few hours later, Ray and Autumn showed their guests to the door.

"Adam is really nice. I hope it works out with Stephanie."

"Yeah, he's a good guy. They're off to a good start."

"Where are the pups?" asked Autumn, peeking into the den. "They're sleeping."

She tiptoed back to the kitchen. Ray helped Autumn clean up and then called Ace to leave. Ace responded immediately, followed by a sleep-heavy Chrissy. They both shook the sleep from their bodies.

Autumn hoped the day would come when they did not have to leave.

⟨⟩

The next day brought thoughts of Beatrice. Autumn's lightened heart made room to try a relationship with her once again. Beatrice was a big part of the reason she had shed her fear, the anger she felt being a catalyst for change. All she felt now was gratitude for the shift and wanted to thank Beatrice for it.

Keeping everyone's opinion of Beatrice in mind, Autumn decided to catch her at the Peabody Foundation office to avoid being alone with her. She entered through the gift shop and looked around. Knowing

114

what the other side of the wall looked like, it was obvious that this area used to be part of the living space of the mansion.

The woman behind the counter greeted Autumn.

"Anything I can help you with?"

Autumn smiled at her. "Can you point me in the direction of Beatrice Peabody's office, please?"

"Sure, up the stairs, first door on the right."

Autumn climbed the stairs. They looked newer than the ones on the other side of the building. It must be part of the renovations to house the Peabody Foundation offices, museum, and gift shop. At the top, the door had Beatrice's name engraved onto a plaque that slid into a frame. The set-up made it easy to change names on the doors in the hallway. She knocked and waited a few beats.

A man opened the door. Autumn recognized him as one of the board members.

"Ms. Clarke, please come in," he said and waved her in, closing the door as he left.

"What do you want?" asked Beatrice, wasting no time on pleasantries.

"Hi, Beatrice. I wanted to check on you and see how you're doing."

"Don't concern yourself."

"We're family. Of course I care."

Beatrice crossed her arms.

"Who was the gentleman that let me in?"

"That was no gentleman. He's a member of the board, Dudley Smith."

"He seemed nice enough."

"Sure, he was thrilled to give me the news that the board voted me out."

"Can they do that?"

"Yes. Under the bylaws, a member can be removed with a two-thirds vote."

Beatrice took a box from the closet and slammed items from the desk into it.

"Did they give you a reason?"

"What's it to you, anyway? Leave me alone!"

"I care about you whether you want me to or not."

Beatrice stopped.

"Why?"

"We're family. Of course I care."

Beatrice let out a heavy sigh.

"They felt that my presence prevented them from moving in positive directions. That I obstruct the vision they have for the foundation. Dudley Smith is the new president."

"But you're the one with the Peabody name."

"It doesn't matter. They want me out. Oxnard would never let them do this to me."

Autumn was quiet, trying to be a calming presence. It was not working. Beatrice kept slamming things into the box.

"Can I do anything to help?"

Through angry tears, Beatrice said, "Yes, you can leave."

Autumn turned away, feeling sorry for Beatrice. The board had taken away the last of her identity. She closed the door gently behind her.

ᑯ෨

Ray got a call from the lab technician.

"The results are in," said the tech. "The skeleton is a positive DNA match to Barbara McCarthy."

Ray hung up and dialed Autumn.

"Your instincts were right," he announced.

"About what?"

"The skeleton is a match for Barbara McCarthy."

"It must be her great-aunt! Do you think Horatio killed her?"

"That's hard to determine from what we know."

"I wish I could find the last page of the diary." Autumn had looked in the hiding places Abigail mentioned, to no avail.

"Maybe it's in the basement."

Autumn rolled her eyes at the thought of tackling that project right now.

"Possibly. All I need is a crew of ten."

"Right, and I don't want anyone outside of us in the basement until this case is closed."

"So, you're volunteering?"

Ray laughed. "I walked into that one!"

"By the way, any word on Barbara?"

"Not yet."

"In the meantime, I'm going to make burial arrangements for Barbara's great-aunt next to the rest of the McCarthy family."

Ray loved Autumn for her kindhearted ways and thoughtful actions. It was then that he realized that he truly loved her with all his heart.

≈ 18 ≈

The next day, Autumn drove at her usual careful pace to Beatrice's house. She got the address from Michael Thornburg and insisted on going over against his warning. She wanted to check on Beatrice after her terrible experience with the Peabody Foundation Board. It was time to put their differences aside. Autumn wanted to try having a relationship with Beatrice one last time.

Chrissy watched her from the car seat. Autumn reached out and pet her.

"I love you, little one."

Chrissy moaned and wagged her tail.

She pulled into Beatrice's driveway. The trimmed shrubbery and ancient trees dominated the front yard of the Tudor Revival house. It was a medium-sized version of the Peabody Mansion. Its grandeur fit Beatrice's self-image. Compared to Oxnard's house, this was more imposing and less formal. Beatrice's gunmetal gray sedan was in the long driveway that wound around the back of the house.

Autumn parked and lifted Chrissy out of her car seat, letting her pause to relieve herself. The flagstone path led to a blue front door with a small leaded glass window at the top. She knocked. After a minute, she banged the brass doorknocker. Nothing.

Beatrice must be home since her car was there. What if something was wrong? Autumn turned the handle and it opened. Cautiously, she and Chrissy stepped over the threshold. Muffled voices drifted down the winding staircase.

"Beatrice?"

No response. Chrissy sniffed the air. Autumn picked her up, not wanting her to wander off. She also did not want a repeat of Chrissy marking a spot over Beatrice's energy. She felt a low grumble in Chrissy's chest.

"What is it, Chrissy?"

"Grrr."

Autumn dialed Ray. It went to voicemail. She whispered a message telling him she was at Beatrice's house and that there might be something wrong. Sounds of a scuffle drifted down the staircase. She hung up as she took the steps two at a time.

Following the sound, she made her way down the hallway. A broom stood in the corner, and she grabbed it, wishing it was a lead pipe instead.

At the end of the hall, a door stood open. Hands clutched Beatrice by the throat, bending her backwards on the bed.

"Hey, get away from her!" Autumn shouted.

She put Chrissy down and grasped the broom handle with both hands ready to do battle.

Beatrice's eyes pleaded for help. Autumn pushed open the door. Greg's hands squeezed tighter blinded by rage.

"I know you killed her!" yelled Greg, shaking Beatrice harder.

Beatrice could not answer, strangling and losing the energy to pry his large hands from her neck. Autumn screamed, "Stop it!" and, with all her strength, slammed the end of the broom handle into Greg's temple. The force woke him out of his frenzy. He let go of Beatrice and started after Autumn. Beatrice buckled forward holding her throat, gulping air.

Autumn backed away. Chrissy barked loud and sharp, mixed with deep growls.

Greg's long stride pounded toward her. He reached out to grab Autumn. She ducked and sidestepped his grasp. Chrissy's bark became more urgent. Autumn hit Greg in the back of the head with the broom handle. It only startled him.

Autumn felt a whoosh of air and a flash of something dark arcing through the air toward Greg's head. She looked in the direction of the projectile and saw a metal bookend smeared with Greg's blood lying on the floor. Beatrice panted with exertion. Greg crumpled to the floor just as heavy footsteps banged up the steps. Chrissy's barking continued.

Autumn and Beatrice looked at each other in shared understanding, too breathless to speak. Autumn scooped Chrissy into her arms, rocking her. The barking stopped, but the low growling continued. Autumn kissed her ear.

"My brave, little girl," she cooed.

Ace charged into the room first, with Ray right behind him. Greg started to regain consciousness, groaning. Ace stood above him, the regal face staring him down, teeth bared and growling, forcing him to stay on the floor.

"Everyone okay?" said Ray.

Beatrice choked, holding her throat. Her raspy breath increased Autumn's concern.

"We need to get both of them to the hospital."

Ray handcuffed Greg before yanking him up, Ace daring him to make a false move.

"I'll take Beatrice to the hospital while you deal with Greg," said Autumn.

Autumn and Beatrice watched as Ray practically dragged Greg down the stairs and threw him in the back-seat of his official vehicle.

Autumn gently guided Beatrice into the back seat of her car since Chrissy's safety seat was in front.

"Just lie down and relax," Autumn said. The red marks on Beatrice's neck were alarming.

She did so without a fight. It was odd to see her so cooperative. Autumn could not tell if she was not speaking because of damage to her throat or because she was in shock.

Beatrice's condition made Autumn push down on the accelerator more than usual. Her focus on getting to the hospital overcame her fear of another fatal accident. Still vigilant of other cars on the road, Autumn got them there in one piece. They went in through the emergency entrance. After registering and seating Beatrice, she asked the receptionist to page Julie Hall. Chrissy quietly snuggled on Autumn's lap.

Julie came walking at a fast pace to where they sat.

"What happened?" She stroked Autumn's arm, the worry pouring from her fingertips.

"I'm okay, just a bit shaken," said Autumn. "Beatrice took the brunt of it. Greg tried to kill her."

"Dear Lord!" Julie exclaimed, as she gently examined her throat. "I'll be right back."

Julie returned in minutes with a nurse who escorted Beatrice to the examination room.

"Thanks, Julie."

"No problem. Now, what happened?"

Autumn took her blow-by-blow through the experience. In reviewing the details, she realized what Greg had said.

"He said, 'I know you killed her.' We need to find out from Beatrice what he meant when she's had a chance to recover."

"In the meantime, Ray's interrogation of Greg should produce some explanation."

"Hopefully. The only things that come out of his mouth are lies."

Julie stroked Chrissy. "You've had a rough day protecting your mommy."

"She was fearless," said Autumn with pride.

Beatrice's nurse waved Julie over. She huddled with Julie for a few minutes before returning to her patient.

Julie sat back down. "You came in just in time. She would have lost consciousness or possibly died."

"I heard the tail-end of an argument before I heard the struggle and ran upstairs."

"Thank goodness you brought her in. She has severe injuries that may cause permanent damage to her voice. Time will tell if she has neurological damage."

"I hope not," said Autumn.

"To be safe, we're keeping her overnight."

"Thanks, Julie. Can I see her before I leave?"

"Only for a minute. I'll watch Chrissy."

Julie had the nurse take Autumn to Beatrice's bed. The woman looked withered, nothing like the belligerent cousin she had come to know. Beatrice gazed at Autumn through slits, clearly exhausted and in pain, the bruises on her neck more prominent than before. Autumn took her hand.

"You're staying here tonight. I'll be back tomorrow to take you home, if you're able." Autumn gently squeezed her frail hand. "Either way, I'll see you tomorrow."

Beatrice blinked.

Back in the waiting room, Autumn asked, "Do you think she'll be discharged tomorrow?"

"I can't make any promises until they assess the extent of the damage."

"You'll keep me posted on her condition?"

"You bet."

Autumn hugged Julie and left.

Her phone rang just as she opened the garage door.

"Hi, Ray. We just got home."

"How's Beatrice?"

"They're keeping her overnight. Greg really took the fight out of her. Speaking of which, how is he?"

"He battled the doctor during the exam. The bruise on his head is the size of an egg."

"Beatrice has good aim. I'm surprised she had the strength to throw that metal bookend at him. Good thing she's a reader."

Ray chuckled.

"What were they fighting about?"

"Beatrice couldn't talk after the fight, so I'm not sure, but Greg yelled 'I know you killed her' while he was choking her."

"Any indication of who he meant?"

"Nope. Maybe Greg can enlighten you."

"I'll try to get it out of him. Right now, we're processing him for two second-degree felony charges: strangulation of Beatrice and attempted assault of you. Each charge carries up to ten years in prison."

"I'm happy to be a witness. Beatrice has the physician's report to corroborate the strangulation."

"Now that Greg turned on her, she may be willing to open up on this dirt-bag."

"Let's hope so."

≈ 19 ≈

Armed with dustpans, brooms, paper towels, rubber gloves, and spray cleaner, Autumn and Stephanie started working at the bottom of the narrow stairs that led down into the cavernous basement of the Peabody mansion. Chrissy sat inside a portable playpen Autumn purchased anticipating the need to keep Chrissy safe while she worked. A few toys and snacks were inside, along with her favorite blanket. She put the comfortable little enclosure close enough that Chrissy could see them but far enough away to prevent dust and debris from getting to her.

"I really appreciate the help, Steph. I'll make it worth your while."

"No problem. I love going through old stuff."

They planned to sweep-up as much dirt from the area as possible before going through the piles of furniture, books, papers, and bric-a-brac. Autumn imagined that whatever the family tired of using they stored down here.

"Have you been to the attic yet?"

Autumn gulped, not having thought about going up there with the basement clean-up heavily weighing on her mind.

"Not yet. There's been so much going on."

"I'm in when you're ready to tackle that space!"

"Great!"

Stephanie swept a pile of dirt into the dustpan and poured it into the trash bag.

"How is Beatrice doing?"

"As of this morning, she can only croak out words. They're keeping her in the hospital at least until tomorrow."

"Boy, Greg really did a number on her. I'm so glad I found Adam before I lost my head with Greg "Bonehead" Manning."

"A new nickname?" Autumn remembered the sound the metal bookend made when it hit Greg's head and cringed.

"Bonehead really refers to my blind desire for him. I'm the bonehead."

Autumn and Stephanie looked at each other and burst out laughing.

"He's a dangerous guy. I'm glad he's in jail."

"Is all the poison out of the basement?" Stephanie asked.

"Ray took what we found in that room. I hope we don't find any more."

Stephanie pulled a broken chair from the pile.

"This must have been nice at some point."

"Let's put all of the broken stuff over here," Autumn said pointing to a corner.

Stephanie opened a box.

"Lots of beautiful dishes!"

Stephanie held up a silver-rimmed china plate with delicate pink roses from one box. Matching glasses filled another box.

"Take them if you like."

"Are you sure?"

"Of course."

Stephanie lugged the boxes upstairs and into her car.

Autumn heard two sets of heavy footsteps coming down the stairs and looked up from sweeping. Ray and Adam came down, followed by Ace and Stephanie.

"We got here just in time. Ms. Muscles over there needed help with the boxes," Adam laughed.

Ray kissed Autumn and went over to pet Chrissy, who was leaping up and down at the sight of Ray. Ace sniffed the playpen and sat next to it.

"You're making good progress, and so am I," said Ray.

"What's going on?" Autumn stopped working to hear his news.

"I stopped by to see Beatrice this afternoon."

"I went this morning. She seems tired."

"She had enough energy to answer my questions by writing on a notepad."

"And?"

"She denies killing Barbara, which is what you'd expect."

"Did she suspect anyone else?"

"No, but she told me that she and Greg had dinner plans the night of the memorial service and she was food shopping when Barbara was supposedly murdered."

"Where's the proof?"

"She gave permission to search her kitchen for the receipt. The amount of items on the list and the time stamp make it unlikely that she had time to shop and put everything away before Greg arrived for dinner at 7 pm."

"That takes us back to square one."

"Except that she drove home past Attic Treasures at the time we estimate the murder to take place and saw a woman wearing a white T-shirt, black skirt, and flat shoes enter the shop."

"Who was it?"

"She only saw her from behind as she drove past. A brunette," said Ray.

"Lots of women in this town are brunette," said Stephanie.

"She also noticed the *open* sign on the door," said Adam.

Autumn thought a moment. "That means whoever that brunette was must have switched the sign to closed, but probably forgot to lock the door."

"Even so, she was the only one that saw anything suspicious. I've talked with the other shop owners on the street, and they didn't notice anything unusual," Adam chimed in.

"I'm going to keep digging," Ray said, and kissed Autumn. "I'll grab a pizza for tonight."

He petted Chrissy and called to Ace as Adam kissed Stephanie goodbye.

"I'll call you when I finish my shift," Adam said to Stephanie.

The men trudged up the steps with Ace in tow.

Autumn saw Stephanie's eyes twinkling and was glad she found someone who made her feel special.

"Okay, back to work! I want this area swabbed and sorted by the end of the day."

"Aye aye, captain!" Stephanie said with a salute.

Their diligence paid off with a small pile of broken furniture and bags of dirt tossed in the rented dumpster, and the organization of boxes of vases and decorative items. The space felt open and clean. There was no sign of a clue in this section of the basement.

≉ 20 ≉

For the first time in months, Autumn and Chrissy walked up the steps to Dr. Wes's office feeling like these visits might become fewer. With each revelation and all of the decisions she made over the past two weeks, her strength grew.

There was no receptionist, but Doctor Wes stood at the desk waiting for them. Autumn pointed to the desk.

"She's on vacation. She and her husband are in Bermuda."

"Nice."

Doctor Wes led them into his office, and they all took their customary seats in the comfortable space. Autumn let out a breath, the couch and Doctor Wes's presence putting her in a state of calm receptivity.

"You did a terrific job at Oxnard's memorial service. The eulogy was sincere and honored his memory."

"Thank you. That means a lot to me."

He looked at Chrissy.

"You were such a good girl at the service."

Chrissy slammed her tail against the sofa cushion.

"How are you two doing in general?

"I've had some major breakthroughs," Autumn said with a proud smile.

"Tell me what's happened."

"First, I cleaned out my parents' bedroom. The veterans' organization picked up their clothes and I'm also donating their furniture."

"How wonderful! What prompted you to do that?"

"In struggling with whether or not to move into the Peabody Mansion, I decided that I love my house and need to make it really mine."

"Your choice of words that it is your house is a major step forward. In the past, you've referred to it as your parents' house."

Autumn pulled in a breath. It was true. The house felt more like hers than it did before.

"Maybe it's because I can see myself there with a family of my own. Ray and Ace like it there, and Chrissy is happy and content. It's big enough for the four of us, or even five, if we have a child."

Doctor Wes nodded.

"Envisioning the next phase of your life and taking steps to make it happen demonstrates healthy progress."

"During the cleanup, I found a letter my dad had written to me."

"What did it say?"

"How he wished he could have told me about being a Peabody and that I should live life on my own terms. He also said to keep an open heart."

"How did you feel after reading the letter?"

"Like he had prepared me for my life and that he wanted me to do what makes me happy. I felt like he trusted me. The letter was a real gift."

"I can see why."

"The letter got rid of feeling betrayed. I'm happy to have a piece of my dad to keep with me."

"Excellent. What an important discovery! It sounds like it went a long way in gaining confidence and knowing what your father wanted for you. That's quite a revelation."

"It is. I'm so grateful."

"What other breakthrough have you had?"

"I'm tired of being a victim of my condition. When Beatrice drove straight at me the other day—"

Doctor Wes's eyebrows went up.

"Excuse me?"

"—She didn't hit us. We were in the car and she came flying around the corner and turned the wheel as if she was going to ram us, and then swerved away. I know she was trying to scare me into a panic attack. It worked for a few minutes, but Chrissy stopped the thoughts, and I recovered faster than ever."

"And then what happened?"

"Then I got angry. Really angry. That's when I knew I've had enough of losing control."

Doctor Wes grinned from ear to ear.

"Anger has two sides. One can be detrimental. The other can be cathartic, bringing about change not able to occur by other means. What happened after you became angry?"

"Oddly, I experienced gratitude toward Beatrice for pushing me past my fear. I went to thank her, but she was upset about getting kicked off the Peabody Foundation Board of Directors, so I left it for the next day."

"Knowing when someone is receptive to the message is an important communication skill. You also put Beatrice's feelings first

126

rather than going with your need to say what you wanted to. These are high-level behaviors."

Autumn smiled, her heart lifted and her mind happy for Doctor Wes's insights.

"I went to her house the next day to check on her. Thank goodness, because Greg Manning was trying to strangle her."

"Oh, no! Why?"

"He thought she'd killed Barbara McCarthy. He was having an affair with her."

"I'm concerned about you putting yourself in danger."

"I called Ray. I couldn't wait until the police got there. She could have been dead by then."

"I see your point. At the same time, caution is called for. Your last investigation almost got you killed."

"You're right. But since I've realized how much Ray and my friends mean to me, I find that my focus is more outward, toward the needs of others. My mom was like that. It feels good to move past my inner fears and try to understand the people around me."

"I'm pleased to hear the outward focus helps you overcome your fears. Sometimes it's important to take care of yourself first, and then others. Please make sure you safeguard yourself going forward."

"I will."

"Your progress is astounding. These last two weeks have propelled you far beyond expectations."

"Leaps and bounds!" said Autumn, doing a little dance on the couch.

Chrissy looked up to see what she was doing and made a grunting sound. Doctor Wes laughed.

"It's giving me energy to work on finding out who killed the person whose skeleton we found at the festival. Turns out, it was Barbara McCarthy's great-aunt."

"Poor Barbara. I read about her death in the paper. I hope the police find the murderer."

"I don't think it was Beatrice, like Greg does. And if he accused Beatrice, then it wasn't Greg like I thought it might be. Ray is on it. You never know, Chrissy may figure it out before he does."

Another round of laughter ensued.

"I'm really pleased with the progress you've made. What do you think about having our sessions once a month instead of every two weeks?"

"Sounds good. I can always call you if I need to see you before then, right?"

"Absolutely."

⚡ 21 ⚡

Beatrice's world upended this past week, her identity stripped from her and any semblance of loyalty in her relationships collapsed. Alienated from her own world, or what she thought was her world,

she now faced a life with no friends, no family, no trust, no purpose, and possible permanent damage to her voice.

Her discharge from the hospital included instructions for taking care of her injury at home. The nurse put her in a wheelchair to take her out of the hospital.

"Wait, I don't have a ride home," she wrote on her little notepad, the full weight of her circumstances hitting her. The only call she could make would be for a taxi.

"Your ride is waiting at the curb," said the nurse.

Puzzled at who it could be, she allowed the nurse to wheel her outside. She could always refuse the ride. The automatic doors slid open. Autumn stood outside of her vehicle with the back door open. Chrissy's head stuck out of the window and gave one welcoming bark when she saw Beatrice. She took advantage of her lack of voice and did not try to say anything. Instead, she allowed Autumn and the nurse to help her into the back-seat.

Autumn thanked the nurse, closed the door, and got into the driver's side.

"How are you feeling?"

Beatrice nodded and touched her throat to indicate that she could not speak.

"That's okay. Just rest. We'll get you home safe and sound."

They pulled away from the curb. Beatrice mentally replayed the day she had tried to cause Autumn to have a panic attack and hoped no one else scared her into one while she sat in the car. Part of her felt remorse for treating Autumn so poorly. She hung her head and looked at her hands.

"I'll bet you're happy to go home and sleep in your own bed."

Beatrice nodded.

"Do you have food in the house?"

Beatrice shook her head, no.

"Let's make a stop at Coleman's Kitchen and get you something good to celebrate getting out of the hospital."

Autumn pulled up to Lisa Coleman's restaurant, ran in and grabbed a menu, and told Beatrice to point to all the things she wanted. List in hand, Autumn ran back inside, and emerged with a fragrant bag full of all of the items Beatrice had requested.

Beatrice felt defeated by kindness. Autumn's gestures gave her hope that there may be a life waiting for her after all. It would just require her to change. A lot. The first step was to give her cousin a chance.

"We're almost home, Beatrice. Do you have the key?"

Beatrice nodded, yes.

They pulled up, and Autumn helped Beatrice out of the vehicle. Then Autumn retrieved Chrissy from her car seat. She shook off and walked alongside Autumn and Beatrice to the front door. Inside, Beatrice looked up the steps and frowned.

"Is the room where I found you the master bedroom?

Beatrice nodded.

"Would you be more comfortable in another room in your house?"

Beatrice shrugged. The thought of being in the room where Greg had attacked her sent shivers up her spine. Just being in this house did not make her feel comfortable, either. She pressed her lips together and shook her head.

"You know, you have other options, like Oxnard's house, or even my house."

Beatrice shook her head to the second offer. She was not ready for that. She mouthed "Oxnard." She let Autumn and Chrissy accompany her upstairs to grab clothes and a toothbrush, then they continued on to Oxnard's house.

They pulled into the driveway. The lawn and shrubs looked at bit shabby without Greg Manning's attention, but did not detract from the home's stately elegance. Beatrice let them in, and Autumn brought the food into the kitchen. Beatrice was glad that the last time she was here she had left the air conditioner on.

She went into the kitchen to find Autumn unpacking the food. Chrissy lapped water from a small glass bowl. Beatrice was surprised that she did not mind having these two in her space.

"Would you like us to stay while you eat? Or do you want to rest?"

Before she could answer, a bang came from upstairs. Autumn told her to stay with Chrissy, and ran to find out what made the noise. Beatrice picked up Chrissy, feeling her tremble against her chest and realized she was the one shaking.

Autumn went to the bottom of the stairs and looked up. Footsteps shuffled behind a door upstairs. She crept up the stairs, listening intently. Her foot landed on a weak tread, and it creaked. She waited. A door off the hallway opened. Autumn cringed, waiting to run. In her mind, she saw an axe-wielding murderer. Her breath caught as the footsteps drew closer.

A white-haired man appeared. He looked puzzled.

"May I help you?" he said gently.

"I'm Autumn Clarke, Oxnard's cousin. Who are you?"

"Jasper Wiggins. I came back to get my things."

Surprised by his presence in the house, Autumn assessed whether or not to be afraid of him. He was a murder suspect, after all. She decided it was best to keep an eye on him.

"Mr. Wiggins, could you please come into the kitchen? Beatrice is here. Come and have something to eat."

"That's very kind of you, miss."

Autumn entered first. When Beatrice saw Jasper Wiggins, her eyebrows went up.

"Mr. Wiggins agreed to join us for lunch," Autumn explained.

Beatrice nodded and sat at the table still holding Chrissy. Autumn was glad that Chrissy had gotten over her dislike of Beatrice. Or maybe she sensed a shift in the way Beatrice felt toward her.

Autumn placed food at each plate. She had not planned to stay, but things just got interesting. She took Chrissy from Beatrice and gave her some chicken from one of the salads.

"Where have you been, Mr. Wiggins?"

He finished chewing a bite of sandwich and swallowed with his eyes downturned.

"I went to a rehab center to stop my drinking habit. Mr. Peabody fired me over it, so I got help. The center got me started, and now I'm required to attend several meetings each week. I was hoping to regain my position here."

"Unfortunately, Oxnard passed away."

Tears welled in his eyes.

"I'm sorry I wasn't here to help him."

He dabbed at his eyes with the napkin.

"I was here. There was nothing to do. He refused treatment and died of thallium poisoning. We believe he was exposed to it at the festival. Do you know anything about that?"

"It must look terrible that I disappeared. Mr. Peabody fired me at the festival. I left there and went directly to rehab. I wish I could be of more help."

Autumn nodded.

"Beatrice has inherited Oxnard's house."

Jasper looked at Beatrice.

"It would be my honor to continue to serve the Peabody family, if you'll have me."

Beatrice's eyes widened. She vigorously nodded.

Jasper Wiggins's face relaxed, and a smile lit his face.

"I'll begin by cleaning up these dishes and grocery shopping. Thank you, miss."

Autumn saw the relief on Beatrice's face.

"By the way, Mr. Wiggins—"

"Please call me Jasper."

"Jasper, Beatrice has had a throat injury and can't speak just yet. Please keep a pad and pen near her."

"I'll take care of it."

"Also, Greg Manning is in jail for harming Beatrice, so we'll need a new landscaper for her house and this property, as well."

Jasper's mouth fell open and quickly closed.

"I'm so sorry to hear that. I'll get right on it."

"I'm glad you're here to help her," said Autumn.

"So am I, miss."

Beatrice nodded.

"Autumn, please."

Chrissy snorted.

"And this is Chrissy. She comforted Oxnard at the end."

Jasper petted her head.

"We're off. I'll check in later, Beatrice."

She mouthed the words thank you.

Once in the car, Autumn dialed Ray and caught him up on the latest developments.

↯ 22 ↯

Despite Autumn's trust, Ray's suspicions regarding Jasper Wiggins led him to confirm that he, in fact, had spent the last few weeks in rehab. The center said he checked in on the afternoon of the festival and stayed until yesterday. By all accounts, Wiggins cooperated with the treatment and worked hard to overcome his addiction. The counselors said that his recovery would be lifelong and that he needed help to stay sober.

Jasper had time before he left the festival to poison the dunk tank, but no one remembered seeing him in the vicinity. Ray kept him on his list of suspects, along with Beatrice.

Greg Manning topped the list, but his attorney blocked Ray from questioning him in jail.

Ray's phone rang. It was Adam Miller.

"Ray, I just got word that Greg Manning made bail."

"His own funds or someone else's?"

"A guy named Dudley Smith. He's the new president of the Peabody Foundation Board of Directors. He also hired the attorney representing Greg."

"Why would he have an interest in Greg?"

"How about I swing by the station and we'll go find out together?"

Ray Reed and Adam Miller pulled up to the Peabody Museum entrance in Ray's unmarked SUV. With Adam in full uniform, no one questioned the nature of their visit. The receptionist directed them to Dudley Smith's office. As they walked down the hall, Ray noticed the absence of a nameplate on Oxnard's former office. He remembered seeing Beatrice's name on the door after Oxnard's death. Once she was fired, he guessed that they removed the sign with her name on it.

Adam knocked on Dudley Smith's door.

"Come in," he called.

Ray went in first. Adam closed the door and stood back, letting Ray ask the questions.

"How can I help you officers?"

"I'm Detective Ray Reed and this is Officer Adam Miller. We'd like to ask you some questions about Greg Manning."

"I bailed him out of jail this morning."

"Why did you do that, Mr. Smith?"

"The poor boy has worked for the Peabody family for years. I couldn't let him stay in prison until his hearing."

"Are you aware of why he was arrested?"

"Of course. He tried to strangle Beatrice. Who hasn't fantasized about that?"

"Are you saying you wished Beatrice Peabody harm?"

"Well, we fired her from our board of directors."

"Making you the new president, correct?"

"That's right. What difference does that make?"

"Did you attend the Peabody Festival?"

"Yes. The entire board membership was present. It's tradition."

"How badly did you want the position of president?"

"It's always been my goal. I've earned it."

"Did you also want Oxnard Peabody removed to clear the way?"

"Oxnard refused to step down. Besides, his family name kept him as a figurehead."

"That doesn't answer my question, Mr. Smith."

"And there will be no more questions without my attorney present."

Outside, Ray and Adam shared their suspicions about Dudley Smith. His casual attitude toward Greg's assault on Beatrice concerned them. His lack of respect for Oxnard called into question his loyalty to the former board president.

Ray dialed Autumn to let her know that Greg Manning made bail.

"Oh no! I'll let Beatrice and Jasper know right away."

"Keep your doors locked."

"Stephanie and I are heading over to the mansion to work in the basement. I'll make sure the doors are locked."

"You'd never hear anyone come in. You didn't hear Adam and me until we were on the stairs."

"I will."

"How about I meet you there and drop off Ace? Greg is scared to death of him."

"With good reason!"

⋘⋙

Ray and Adam pulled up in two vehicles. Autumn, Chrissy, and Stephanie greeted their guys and Ace. Autumn took Ace's leash and gave Ray a key in case he needed to get back in.

"I spoke to Jasper, and he promised me he'd keep an eye out for Greg and call me if he shows up," Autumn said.

"For all we know, Jasper is in on it with Greg. They both had access to the thallium and both had opportunity to poison the dunk tank at the festival," said Ray.

"I could go to Beatrice's house and sit outside," said Adam.

"Good idea. Let them know you're outside and see if you can get any information from those two. Just because Greg attacked Beatrice doesn't mean she didn't have a hand in her brother's death. She certainly had motive," said Ray.

"Will do."

Adam waved goodbye, promising Stephanie he would be careful.

Ray kissed Autumn, petted Ace, and drove off.

Autumn locked the front door, pulling on it to make sure it was secure.

In the basement, they set Chrissy in the playpen with Ace on a cushion beside her close to the basement steps. They left the basement door slightly ajar so the canines could hear any activity upstairs. Stephanie and Autumn started working in the room where Autumn had found the photo album and Ray discovered the thallium.

"Let's be extra careful in here. There might be traces of thallium left behind."

They pulled on thick rubber gloves and got to work. This room contained books, more photo albums, and children's toys. Stephanie lifted a doll by the leg. Dirt crusted the face and its one arm sought out a hug.

"I think this can go into the trash pile."

"I agree. Dolls creep me out, anyway. For the toys, only keep the rocking horse and the playhouse. They can be restored," said Autumn.

The trash pile grew faster than the keep pile.

"I hope these books are salvageable," said Autumn.

She dipped a clean cloth into book-cleaning gel purchased online. She selected a leather volume, blew the dust off it, and gently wiped a corner. A bright burgundy color emerged from the grime. Confident with the results, she worked at the rest of the cover.

"Like new!" Autumn held up her work.

"That's amazing. Now to get the musty smell out of them."

"I read that a sock filled with rice or cat litter will absorb the smell. So will fabric softener sheets between the pages. That will be the next phase."

"It's a shame that Barbara can't be here to enjoy the book-discovery portion of the cleanup."

"I hear that Barbara's family put the store on the market. I believe she also owned the building."

"We need to keep that place open. I hope we get someone as knowledgeable as Barbara in there."

Autumn turned over the book and shook it to see if any loose pages fell out. She did this with each book, and then carefully stacked them in a box to take upstairs. There were old textbooks, books on philosophy, science, and religion, and novels from the early twentieth century. Some of the hardbacks had gilded lettering and beautiful illustrations.

The next book in the pile was titled, *Open Confessions*, by Agnes Humphrey. Using a slightly damp cloth, Autumn cleaned the blue dust jacket, and then flipped the pages to see if anything came out. A page with a ragged edge floated to the ground.

"Steph, look!"

"What is it?"

Abigail's familiar handwriting stood out from the page. The tattered edge looked as though someone had torn it from its binding. They huddled together reading the final entry from Abigail's diary:

> Horatio's affairs have been many, but never before has it occurred in my own home. I discovered him sleeping with one of the staff. The humiliation is beyond what I have suffered to this point. How many others know?
>
> She was a trusted member of my household. Horatio refused to fire her, so I dealt with it myself. When Horatio found out what I had done, he had no choice but to bury her in the field. We told the rest of the staff she had left our employ to care for her sick mother. By their faces, I saw they did not believe it, but they said nothing.
>
> His anger makes me afraid of what he will do next. I must leave this place.

Autumn's hand covered her mouth. Stephanie's just hung open. They looked at each other.

"Abigail Peabody killed Ann McCarthy!" Autumn said, trying to catch her breath.

"It wasn't Horatio Peabody!"

"I feel so much better knowing that I don't have a murderer for a great-grandfather!"

"No wonder he drank!"

They burst out laughing. Not that murder was funny, but when it comes to relatives, the lesser evils are preferred.

Nothing could beat the discovery of the final diary page, so they hauled the trash and books up the stairs, swept the floor, and decided to call it a day.

With Chrissy and Ace, they lounged in the living room enjoying the wooded view from the Palladian window.

"What do you think happened to Abigail?" asked Stephanie.

"We need to trace her family in the Hudson River Valley to see what we can find out."

"Maybe they lied about Abigail never making it to their house."

"It's possible."

The front door opened, and Ace stood at attention. Ray called out and Ace went running, bringing him back to the living room. Chrissy's tail went wild at the sight of Ray. He petted her and rubbed her belly.

Looking at the dirt-smudged young women, Adam laughed. "You ladies need to get cleaned up."

"I guess we are kinda grungy," said Stephanie.

"We will, but first our news. We found the last page of Abigail's diary!" said Autumn.

"She found it," corrected Stephanie.

"And?" Ray waited

"Abigail killed Ann McCarthy, not Horatio!"

"Incredible. You never know what someone is capable of given the right circumstances. I guess she had had enough," said Ray.

"Now all I have to do is find out if she made it to New York after it happened."

"You can't do research on an empty stomach. Adam and I will take you to dinner."

"Okay. Pick us up in an hour at my place," said Autumn.

Stephanie dropped Autumn and Chrissy at their house and went home to shower and change.

Autumn took a shower and put on a tank top and jeans. She brushed Chrissy and used the rhinestone clips as the finishing touch on her pretty little girl.

The gang showed up and they went to dinner at a BYOB Italian place on Main Street. They sat at an outdoor table with a huge green umbrella, and enjoyed dinner. The pups ate their dinners in the shade next to the table.

"We got so much done today, I'm going to take Stephanie on a thank-you excursion," said Autumn.

"Where?" Stephanie asked, excitement in her voice.

"You'll see soon enough."

"I don't want to spoil such a great evening, but please remember that Greg Manning is lurking out there somewhere. Be careful," said Ray.

Adam nodded his agreement.

"We will. He'd be stupid to do anything to us in public," said Stephanie.

"With this character, you never know," said Adam.

⚡ 23 ⚡

The heat finally broke, and a warm breeze encouraged people out of air-conditioned spaces. Stephanie picked up Autumn and Chrissy with all the windows down.

"Where are we going?" asked Stephanie.

"Head toward Main Street."

When they got close, Autumn pointed to a parking spot. Stephanie pulled in. She looked up. They were in front of Jade's Jewelry. She looked at Autumn, who smiled and nodded.

The three of them walked into Jade's and spotted her behind the counter.

"How can I help you lovely ladies?"

"My friend doesn't know what she wants yet," said Autumn.

"I have some new things in the back," said Jade.

"Okay if I put Chrissy down?"

"Sure," Jade said, disappearing into the back.

Autumn put Chrissy down and took her off the leash. Chrissy sniffed around the counter and then made her way behind the counter while a long silver necklace embedded with sparkling gems distracted Autumn and Stephanie.

A few minutes passed before they heard, "What are you doing back here, cutie pie?"

Autumn went running to grab Chrissy and found her in the back with Jade.

"Sorry about that," said Autumn.

"No harm done," Jade said. She held a tray of choice pieces to show Stephanie.

Autumn hugged Chrissy and whispered in her ear, "Stay near me, sweetheart."

Nausea overwhelmed Autumn and the room spun as her perspective shifted. She found herself looking up on a shelf in the backroom. On it, a mannequin head sported a brunette wig that looked like the description of the woman Beatrice gave Ray.

She regained her focus, kissed Chrissy's ear, and whispered "Good girl."

Stephanie was deep into the search for her prize, bejeweled from ears to fingers.

"This baby needs a little walk. I'll be right back."

Stephanie said *okay* without looking up. Jade was into it as much as Stephanie.

Autumn left the shop and walked Chrissy to the corner and down the alleyway before calling Ray. Despite a lack of patrons on Main Street today, she wanted to make sure the conversation did not travel into random public ears.

"You'll never guess what Chrissy found," she said.

"What?"

"A brown wig matching Beatrice's description of the woman who went into Attic Treasures."

"Where did she find it?"

"Jade's Jewelry. We're here now. I'm outside on the corner. Stephanie is picking out her thank-you gifts. She has no idea about the wig."

"How long will you be there?"

"At this rate, until Stephanie has tried on everything in the store."

"I'll follow-up with her this afternoon. It could be just coincidence."

"Maybe, but the odds are in favor of her as a strong suspect. She has proximity to the victim and was angry at Barbara's attention toward Greg."

"I hear you."

Autumn gasped, Chrissy let out a sharp bark, and the phone went dead.

☾☽

Stephanie held up a sparkling blue topaz necklace and compared it to a turquoise and jade necklace. The contrast between the shine of the cut topaz versus the opaque color of the natural stones created a quandary. Her relationship with Adam made her feel more grounded than ever before, so her attraction to the blue and green stones of the second necklace felt right. It was time to try something new. It also had matching earrings and a ring, all set in silver.

A bang on the door and urgent barking startled her from her decision. She placed the necklaces on the counter and went to the door. Chrissy panted between barks. Stephanie had never seen her so stressed.

"Where's your mommy?"

Autumn would never leave Chrissy alone.

Chrissy barked again and went back out to the sidewalk, glancing over her shoulder at Stephanie.

Jade came to the door.

"Everything all right?"

"I don't know. I don't see Autumn. I'll be back."

Stephanie followed Chrissy to the corner. Autumn's cell phone lay on the ground. She picked it up. Chrissy looked down the street and barked again. Stephanie could not see anything.

She dialed Adam and asked him to get hold of Ray, telling him she would follow Chrissy down York Avenue. She held Chrissy's leash and went where Chrissy pulled her. Two blocks down, there was nothing but shops in between townhouses. Chrissy smelled the ground and continued forward.

A warehouse loomed up ahead; its rusty metal roof and dull red paint seemed to add to the urgency Stephanie felt. Chrissy strained against the leash, and then stopped at the wood door with a barred window at the top. She gazed up the side of the building. Plywood covered most of the windows; bars covered the rest.

Chrissy's high-pitched barking came in rapid rhythm to Stephanie's heartbeat. She reached out to try the door lever, its flat finish reflecting her sense of foreboding, and pressed down. It clicked and the door creaked open, Chrissy ready to launch into the shadows beyond. Stephanie held her back.

Her nerves sent alarm bells through her body. Should they wait for Ray and Adam? By then it could be too late. She told Chrissy to be quiet. Chrissy went silent. Stephanie crept into the dim space. The door closed behind her, darkness wrapping around them. She stopped, letting her eyes adjust. Her ears perked up, listening for what her eyes could not see. She heard a shuffling sound to her right just before everything went black.

CB&O

Adam and Ray crawled down York Avenue in the police cruiser, inspecting every alleyway. Ace rode in the back, vigilant for sights, sounds, and smells. They stopped the occasional pedestrian to see if they had seen anything. No luck.

Jade told them neither Stephanie nor Chrissy had come back to the shop.

"They couldn't have gone too far," said Adam.

"Right," Ray said, his eyes watchful for signs of movement.

As they passed the old warehouse door, the clean spot on an otherwise filthy door indicated someone recently entered the aban-

141

doned space. It was a red alert to Ray, calling him to look inside the building.

Adam pulled to the side of the narrow street. The two cautiously emerged from the vehicle, looking up and around making sure no one could launch a surprise attack. Ray opened the door for Ace, who bounded toward the steel door and let out his deep, authoritative bark. As they got closer, they heard whimpering behind the door. Ray flung it open to see Chrissy, crying and dirty. He picked her up while Adam drew his gun. Ace sniffed her to make sure she was okay.

"We're definitely warm," said Ray petting Ace. "Good boy."

Ace went in behind Adam and ahead of Ray.

Adam quietly searched their immediate surroundings, hypervigilant to sound and shining his flashlight through the shadows. Support beams and equipment provided hiding places for the perpetrator. He followed the scuffmarks left in the thick dirt on the floor. Ace tracked the scent and passed Adam, able to see clearly in the murky light.

Ray stayed back, holding Chrissy tight. He put his forehead against hers and whispered, "Show me what happened."

Nausea overtook him and the world spun out of control. A moment later, his vision took on a new perspective. From a low angle, he saw the scene through Chrissy's eyes. First on the street, where Chrissy spotted Greg Manning coming toward Autumn and then watched as he dragged her down the street, his hand over her mouth.

Then Chrissy showed him how Stephanie entered the warehouse and an unidentifiable figure hit Stephanie and carried her off into the depths of the building.

The visions subsided, and he made a dizzying transition back to his own perspective. He hugged Chrissy close and said, "Good girl." She whimpered, and he stroked her back. "We'll find your mommy and Aunt Stephanie."

Ray debated putting Chrissy in the police car, but the heat made him wary of her safety. He put her down, threaded his hand through the leash handle, and drew his gun. She quietly walked with him.

A clang came from overhead. Adam and Ace raced up the metal steps. Ray proceeded more slowly to see if the sound was a distraction. He knew that Autumn and Stephanie were either unconscious or subdued, so they could not make a sound; otherwise the two of them would make a racket. He quickened his step toward the stairs and saw a dark figure moving slowly at the other end of the vast room. Ray gestured to Chrissy to stay.

He closed the gap between the unknown man and himself with long strides. The suspect jumped at Ray's presence, but Ray had his handcuffs out and around the man's wrists before he knew who it was. Grabbing him by the arm, Ray pulled him toward the back door and opened it to let in some light.

Dudley Smith frowned at Ray.

"Where are Autumn and Stephanie, Mr. Smith?" Ray growled.

Dudley Smith's mouth opened and closed, but no sound came out. Ray heard Ace barking upstairs. Chrissy started barking in reply. He yanked his suspect and forced him up the metal steps. At the top, Adam held Greg Manning at gunpoint. Ace bared his teeth and growled.

"The girls are in a room back there," Adam directed Ray with his head.

Ray plopped Dudley onto a ripped chair.

"Don't move, Mr. Smith."

Ray took Adam's handcuffs and secured Greg.

"You're both under arrest for assault and kidnapping," said Ray.

Adam read them their rights. Ace stood at attention letting out a low growl warning them not to try anything.

"Keep that dog away from me!" Greg yelled.

Ray chuckled to himself and let Ace have some fun while he went to retrieve the women.

Chrissy made it to the top of the stairs and ran toward where the men held Autumn and Stephanie captive. Ray untied Autumn first. Blood trickled down her arm from a shallow cut near her shoulder. Autumn seemed unaware that she was bleeding and reached out toward Chrissy, who leapt into her arms and grunted excitedly between licks.

Stephanie threw the ropes down and removed the tape carefully from her mouth, revealing a purple bruise.

"How dare they do this to us? I'm pressing charges!" she said, lightly touching the back of her head. Fury oozed from every pore. "One of them hit me on the head!"

"And the face. We need to get you to the hospital," said Ray, examining the bump on Stephanie's head and pressing gently on the darkened skin near her mouth.

Autumn hugged Chrissy tight and kissed her head.

"I'm so glad you're okay, my smart little girl!"

They walked back to where a forlorn Dudley Smith hung his head.

"Mr. Smith?" said Autumn. "What are you doing here?"

"Are you kidding me? All of this was his idea!" screamed Greg. "He hired me to kill Oxnard! Swore no one would figure out who did it."

"Shut up, you idiot!" said Dudley Smith, finally finding his voice.

Ray decided to take advantage of Greg's desire to share.

"Did Beatrice have anything to do with Oxnard's death?"

"She fantasized about his death but would never go through with it, even when I tried to convince her to let me handle it for her," confessed Greg.

"How did you administer the poison, Mr. Manning?" asked Ray.

"Poured a bunch of those bottles of thallium into the dunk tank. It was easy." Greg looked proud

of his idea.

"You put a lot of people at risk! Did you think of that?" Stephanie closed the gap between herself and her captor.

"Oxnard was the only one going in the tank," he said, raising his chin in defiance.

"How about Jasper Wiggins?"

"He's a useless drunk. I'm surprised Oxnard kept him as long as he did. No, he just wanted to keep his job."

"Why kidnap Autumn?" asked Ray

"She kept poking her nose into everything," Greg said. then turning to Autumn, he asked, "What do you care about Beatrice, anyway? She hates you!"

"She's family," Autumn said simply.

"Your death would have looked like an accident if your friend hadn't shown up," Greg spat, his anger unable to contain the damning words falling from his mouth.

"You're dumber than I thought," said Stephanie. "What possible reason would Autumn have to go into this warehouse? Besides, she never would have left Chrissy alone."

"Stupid dog," Greg grumbled.

"Smarter than you," said Autumn, smiling.

"Why were you here, Mr. Smith?" asked Adam.

"Greg called and asked me to meet him here so we could talk."

"About what?" ask Ray.

Dudley Smith, shut down. "I want an attorney."

"You'll get one," Ray promised.

∞

With Ray, Ace, and Adam hauling Greg and Dudley to the police station, Autumn and Stephanie headed to the emergency room. The doctor gave her an ice pack, some mild pain medication, and advice to rest.

"You never got your gift. Did you figure out what you want?" asked Autumn.

"Yes, but we don't need to get anything. Today's adventure put my priorities in order."

Autumn looked gratefully at Stephanie.

"I owe you more than some jewelry," said Autumn

"For what?"

"You saved my life, and it almost cost you yours," said Autumn, tears welling.

Stephanie hugged her.

"There was no way I was letting anything happen to you."

"We're still going shopping at some point. Let's head home for now. I need a shower and so does Chrissy."

"A shower sounds wonderful."

CB&O

A long, warm shower for Chrissy and Autumn cleaned most of the stress from them. The weather allowed them to sit outside and enjoy the sunshine. Chrissy lay on a beach towel between Autumn's legs on the lounge chair, air-drying. Autumn combed her long locks so she would dry more quickly. Autumn's own hair required the blow dryer to combat frizz.

She looked down and saw the exhaustion in Chrissy's deep brown eyes.

"You saved me, little girl," she cooed.

Chrissy grunted and closed her eyes. Autumn grinned as Chrissy snored contentedly. They were safe. Autumn followed her into dreamland.

The ringtone on her cell phone startled them both awake. She looked at the time. They had been asleep for about an hour. Chrissy stretched on her side as Autumn answered the phone.

"Did I wake you?" asked Ray.

"It's okay. We fell asleep outside."

"You needed the rest after what you've been through."

"Is Greg behind bars?"

"Yes, with no opportunity for bail. Dudley Smith made bail and is scheduled for his court appearance next week."

"Even after what Greg told us?"

"Dudley has a right to tell his side of the story."

"I'm going to call Beatrice and let her know what's been going on. She'll be glad that Greg is back in jail."

"Do you want Ace and me to pick up some dinner and come over?"

"That would be great. I don't feel like cooking."

"See you in a while, then."

She hung up and dialed Beatrice. Jasper answered the phone, saying that Beatrice still had difficulty speaking.

"Please tell her that Greg is back in jail."

He relayed the message.

"She looks relieved."

"Also, tell her that Dudley Smith was arrested for scheming with Greg Manning."

"I've never seen her smile like that before," said Jasper.

"Good. Things are going to get better from here."

"Yes, ma'am."

⊰∙⊱

When Jade heard about Greg Manning's arrest, she closed up her shop and went to the county jail.

The sight of her sent Greg into a tizzy.

"What are you doing here, Jade?"

"I heard they had you locked up in this awful place and wanted to help."

Her bleached-blonde hair practically glowed against her navy blue short-sleeved shirt. A shimmering necklace cascaded from her neck to her ribcage.

"I have enough to worry about. We've been over for a long time."

"But I did it for you!"

"What did you do?"

"Got rid of Barbara McCarthy. She really appreciated the salad I brought her. She dug right in. Too bad she couldn't tell water hemlock from a regular parsnip. Lucky for me, I found some growing along the stream a couple of miles from town."

"Why would you kill Barbara?" exclaimed Greg.

"I did it for you, for us."

"There is no us! I almost killed Beatrice because I thought she was the one."

"Beatrice doesn't have the chutzpah to do something like that. That's why we're perfect together."

Greg put his head in his hands.

Ray peeked around the doorway.

"Is that why there's a brown wig in your shop, Ms. Fisher?"

Jade gasped. Ray had heard the entire conversation.

"You just made my job much easier."

"Maybe I was lying," said Jade, nose in the air.

"We found hairs in Attic Treasures that match the wig. My tech was there almost all night looking for that one piece of missing evidence. You're under arrest for the murder of Barbara McCarthy."

≈ 24 ≈

Autumn drove down Main Street. Chrissy enjoyed having the windows down and the late-September breeze blowing against her face. Jade's Jewelry had a *closed* sign on it, the display window empty of its bounty. Jade's sister from Florida liquidated the store's contents and sold Jade's house to pay her attorney bills and put some aside for Jade to use as needed.

Jade Fisher sat in jail awaiting trial for the first-degree murder of Barbara McCarthy. The news sent a shockwave through Knollwood. She was in the same boat as Greg Manning, with the district attorney anticipating life sentences for both. Too bad they were in separate prisons. Her fantasy of being with Greg would need to stay in her imagination.

The lights were on at Attic Treasures, although the name now read *Stacey's Vintage Books*. The bell jingled as Chrissy and Autumn walked onto a new black-and-white tile floor that gave the illusion of expanded space. The shop smelled of fresh paint, furniture polish, and a hint of sage. The bookshelves glowed and the book categories were reorganized. The space felt open and made Autumn want to linger. A sign for the rare-books room hung over the doorway that used to say *employees only*. The counter glass gleamed. The new owner had strategically tucked comfortable chairs covered in antique yellow fabric into private corners, creating intimate spaces to read.

A woman of about four feet ten came out from behind one of the shelves. She looked familiar. Her short, sandy-colored hair and bright smile welcomed Autumn. Her miniature poodle came prancing over to Chrissy. They wagged their tails and sniffed, becoming instant friends.

"Hi, I'm Stacey Eldridge and this is Clay."

Autumn shook her hand and petted Clay.

"I'm Autumn Clarke-Peabody, and this is Chrissy. Welcome to the neighborhood!"

She pulled a box of expensive chocolates from her giant tote bag and handed it to Stacey.

"I love chocolate! Thank you." Stacey stashed them behind the counter then looked at Chrissy. "She's adorable. It's nice that Clay made a friend."

"There are lots of dogs in this town. I can bring a few of my friends here with their dogs so Clay can get acquainted."

"I'd appreciate that."

"The place looks great."

"Thank you. It had good bones, but felt too dark for me. Yellow is my favorite color," Stacey said looking pleased as she gazed at the finished product.

Autumn was not surprised. Yellow matched Stacey's sunny disposition.

"I see your book offerings are extensive. How are your records about town history?"

"Actually, I grew up in this town, but my family moved away when I was in tenth grade. I was Stacey Kendrick back then."

"I remember you! You were the editor of the school paper and president of the Knollwood Historical Society Club."

"Right! Knollwood history was my favorite hobby. We moved up to New Hope. I finished high school there and met my husband. Unfortunately, he passed away a few months ago."

"Oh, I'm sorry to hear that."

"He had a good life insurance policy, so I came back here and saw the bookstore for sale. It's always been my dream to own one. It's a shame what happened to the former owner."

"Yes, it is. We'll miss her. But it's nice having the store continue in this town. I own the Peabody Mansion. There are tons of antique books in that place if you want to come take a look."

Stacey rubbed her hands together. "Oh, boy, nothing like a good book hunt."

"Let's make a date to do that. I'm also a member of the Knollwood Chamber of Commerce. Have you registered yet?"

"That's a marvelous idea."

"Great. Well, I have to run, but we'll see you soon." Autumn took a business card from the counter.

Stacey petted Chrissy goodbye and hugged Autumn.

Their next stop was Lisa's café. She picked up a variety of sandwiches and desserts for a picnic with Ray, Chrissy, and Ace at Willow Lake. She purchased pet food and treats elsewhere. It was Ray's idea for them to take a day off and relax. Willow Lake's trails and picnic areas made for a perfect day together with the pups.

Ray picked them up in his SUV. Autumn secured Chrissy in the backseat with Ace and went around the back to load the picnic basket in the storage area. She pushed around blankets, towels, balls, and a cooler. She opened the lid. Ray had filled it with water, beer, iced tea, and wine.

"Couldn't decide what you felt like drinking?" teased Autumn as she pulled the passenger door closed.

"Well, the water is for the pups. I covered the bases for us." He smiled.

The tree-lined entrance to the park cooled off the day. Only a few cars sat in the parking lot, as it was the middle of the week and kids were back in school. Birds chirped and an occasional dog barked. The wind rustled the leaves as they unpacked their picnic.

They chose chilled white wine with their gourmet sandwiches. They toasted Lisa and her culinary skills and then raised a glass to their future. The iced tea went well with their layered dessert. It was all delicious. The pups chowed down on their snacks, drank water, and ran around nudging the ball between them. Autumn and Ray stretched out on the blanket.

"It doesn't get better than this," said Ray. "I've never been happier."

"I didn't think it was possible to feel this comfortable with anyone. Everything feels right when we're together," Autumn said, her eyes closed.

"I'm glad you said that," said Ray, reaching into his pocket. He lifted himself onto one knee and opened the red velvet box. "Autumn."

"Mmm?"

"Open your eyes."

She squinted and saw Ray kneeling before her. She pushed herself into a sitting position, the sunlight glinting off a large diamond in a white gold setting.

"I know we've only been together a short time, but I've never felt like this about anyone."

Autumn's hand went to her heart.

"When I think that you could have died at the hands of Greg Manning and Dudley Smith, it rips me up inside. I can't stand the thought."

"Neither can I," she joked.

"I want to be with you always, to care for you and protect you. Will you marry me?"

Autumn let out a squeal and wrapped herself around him, kissing him deeply.

"I love you so much. Yes, yes, yes!"

The dogs came running over and demanded they be included in the hug. The four of them became a mass of arms, legs, fur, and tails in a tangle of joy. Ray still held the box. He got the pups to sit down.

"Give me your hand."

Autumn held out her hand, and Ray lovingly slipped the ring on her finger. He embraced her, his love warming her heart and lifting her spirits. He pushed her away to look into her eyes.

"Now I can officially help you redecorate the house," he said smiling.

"You mean *our* house."

⋘⋙

They held their engagement party in the yard of their home despite the renovations in progress. All of the neighbors, their pups, the members of the Peabody Foundation, Stephanie and Adam, Maureen Roberts, Stacey Eldridge and Clay, and Beatrice and Jasper attended. Ray's parents came in from out of town. They instantly loved Autumn and chatted as if they had known each other for years.

Autumn knew it was the right decision to keep her parents' home as their primary residence and make it their own. Chrissy got to laze in her familiar places and enjoyed a change of scene with her regular visits to the Peabody Mansion.

Maureen's disappointment over Autumn's decision to keep her parents' house was short-lived when she learned of the renovation efforts and Ray's enthusiasm for home improvement.

The twinkle lights Ray strung across the yard looked beautiful once the sun went down. Autumn and Ray lit candles on each table and up lit the trees. It looked romantic.

Autumn called a local caterer with a full staff for the party so that Lisa could come and enjoy herself.

Chrissy was in a corner of the yard entertaining Mickey, Ace, Teddy, and Clay. Despite Clay's tiny stature, he got along well and held his own in a game of ball. Bowls filled with snacks, food, and water stood on a special slate patio Autumn had designed just for Chrissy's guests.

Everyone barraged Autumn and Ray with questions about the wedding. The Peabody Mansion was to be the location, with the date set for one year away in October, the weekend before Halloween. Stephanie's role as maid of honor allowed her to answer many of the questions about the ceremony and such.

Autumn gazed across the lawn and saw Beatrice speaking — well, mostly listening — with a couple of the board members. She actually smiled, and Autumn knew that the attack had transformed Beatrice into a kinder person. Over one of their many coffees either in Beatrice's or Autumn's kitchen, Beatrice told Autumn that in a way she was glad it happened. Autumn and Chrissy's heroics made her realize that she had someone in her corner. Having PTSD herself from the experience made Beatrice regret the stunt she pulled trying to push Autumn into a panic attack. Autumn recommended she see Dr. Wes, and Beatrice agreed.

She watched a sober Jasper Wiggins talking with Maureen Roberts, their heads together as though planning a heist. They seemed quite cozy.

Adam tapped his glass and the rest chimed in, signaling a kiss from the engaged couple. They happily complied.

⚥ 25 ⚥

With Greg Manning in jail, likely to get a life sentence without parole for the first-degree murder of Oxnard Peabody, strangulation of Beatrice Peabody, and the assault and kidnapping of Autumn and Stephanie, Autumn could relax and realize her vision of the pet-friendly Peabody Mansion Bed & Breakfast. Thankfully, Lisa Coleman agreed to be the breakfast chef. Autumn's vision did not include cooking a mediocre breakfast for her guests when they could have a fabulous one prepared by Lisa. Additionally, Autumn's offer for Lisa to take a room in the vendor's row section of the recreation area and offer premade sandwiches and baked goods met with enthusiasm, especially when Autumn refused any rent. The plan was to hire a clerk to operate the space so Lisa could maintain her primary location.

A crew was busy cleaning up the basement under Autumn's direction for the keep, donate, and trash items. The contractors would come next to create the recreation center she and Ray were designing for the basement. It included his dream of a two-lane bowling alley, a game room, and a movie theater, both for himself and for guests staying at the Peabody Mansion.

The annual Peabody Festival drew guests wanting to stay in the place where the Peabody family had once lived and to learn about them at the museum in the same building. The ten bedrooms were already booked starting next June, giving her time to put final touches on the guest rooms. The wedding scheduled for next October gave them plenty of time to plan.

Stephanie was at the helm of the wedding plans. She and Autumn discussed it in detail, and then Stephanie insisted on taking over, which was fine with Autumn. No one was better qualified than her best friend to know what she wanted, from flowers to food to cake. They agreed to shop for the wedding dress together and already booked appointments at several nearby bridal salons. Stephanie insisted on buying it no more than six to nine months in advance.

Working with Stacey on tracking down one of Abigail's last remaining relatives brought them closer. She was smart and strategic, earning Autumn's admiration. Stacey's sweet voice convinced Abigail's great niece to share the family history. Abigail had made it to the Hudson River Valley in New York, where the family protected their own by playing into the disappearance story. She changed her name and stayed under the radar, living out her life with as much freedom as guilt allows.

Autumn hired Stacey to create a display with the old photos, dedicated to the staff of the mansion and highlighting the important role they had played, especially Ann McCarthy. Autumn decided that Abigail Peabody's diary and confession should be part of a special display in the museum. After all, it was a historical mystery solved that would likely be of interest to visitors. And it exonerated Horatio Peabody. She authorized the installation and trusted Stacey to do it in good taste.

Stacey wanted to open an annex to the bookshop as part of vendor's row in the newly renovated basement at the Peabody mansion. It would feature some of the books Autumn found in the cellar. Stacey had already earmarked several rare volumes for the museum as part of a Peabody collection display. A few went into Stacey's shop, with the rest shelved in new bookcases Autumn commissioned for the main mansion's library room.

Dudley Smith awaited trial, and likely conviction on conspiracy to commit murder with Greg Manning would send him to jail for life. It also left a vacancy for the president's chair.

Autumn became president of the Peabody Foundation by unanimous vote, ensuring the integrity and focus that Oxnard had brought to the role. She hoped to attract additional tourism to Knollwood and the surrounding areas. Beatrice was surprisingly fine with it. Autumn campaigned to have her reinstated to the board and won. Even though Beatrice could only talk for short periods, her voice improved with each passing week.

Beatrice retained Jasper Wiggins as house manager, living in Oxnard's residence, to his utter delight. She found it difficult to go into her stone Tudor with the memory of Greg choking her. On Autumn's recommendation, Beatrice called Maureen Roberts, who was delighted to sell it and, after a bidding war, fetched a price above what Beatrice was asking.

Autumn and Chrissy snuggled with Ray and Ace on the couch in their living room.

"Are you happy in your job?"

Ray looked puzzled. "Sure, why?"

"If you want, you can quit your job and work with me at the B&B. We make a great team."

Ray paused before answering.

"That's a generous offer, but I like what I do. I'm thinking of maybe trying for police chief."

"You'd make a great police chief!"

"You know I'll help at the mansion any way I can, but right now, I don't see it as my main work."

"I understand. That's fine. It's an open invitation."

He nodded and hugged her.

"You know, I still haven't been up in the attic. There are so many projects happening at once. We need to go up there soon."

"Fine with me. You never know what valuables we might discover. Maybe even another mystery."

Autumn squeezed the arm he had wrapped around her waist and petted Chrissy and Ace.

"My most valuable treasures are right here with me."

Book Club Questions
The Dog-Eared Diary: A Chrissy the Shih Tzu Mystery

1. When Autumn finds out her true lineage, she felt betrayed, despite the rewards. Would you have felt the same or differently?

2. Stephanie seems to like the wrong kind of guy. Do you know anyone like that? What did you think of her ultimate choice of a boyfriend?

3. In the story, Autumn goes through her dad's clothing and gives some of the best pieces to Ray. Would you give your boyfriend your father's clothing? What did you think of Autumn doing that?

4. How do you feel about Autumn giving so much emphasis to Ray's input about which house she and Chrissy should live in without a more committed relationship between herself and Ray?

5. How do you think Beatrice formed such a regal and uppity view of herself? Why did Oxnard not have the same view of himself?

6. Could a heavy-drinking and cheating spouse drive you to kill the lover of your cheating spouse? Why or why not?

7. What do you think of Beatrice's transformation? What did you think of the way Autumn treated her? How would you have responded to Beatrice?

8. What did you think about Autumn's choice of where to live? What would you have done?

9. Did the characters act and respond in ways that seemed natural or familiar to you? Why or why not?

10. Which character did you most identify with? Why?

11. Which was your least favorite character?

12. What surprised you most about this story?

13. What part of the story was most compelling to you?

14. How would you describe the roles of the canine characters in the plot?

15. Did you think you knew the identity of the murderer of Oxnard before it was revealed? Were you correct? What was your first clue?

16. Did you find the ending surprising or predictable? Why?

17. How did PTSD influence the characters and plot development?

18. Do you think the events depicted in this story could actually happen? Explain.

19. Would *Chrissy's Mysteries* interest you as an original TV series?

20. If you were to keep the same secret as Oxnard did about a family member, would you break the promise if said family member made you fear for your life?

21. With all the food mentioned in the book, which sounded the most appetizing, and which dish would you like to make?

About the Author

Diane Wing, M.A. grew up in a household where her vivid imagination could thrive. Crafting short stories and poetry from an early age, writing remained part of her life throughout her 25-year corporate career. Her training in clinical psychology shows up in her characters' struggles and in her non-fiction books about energetic consciousness, tarot, and happiness. Diane seeks to help the reader find the flame of their own unique path sparked by her stories and insights for personal growth.

Diane is an avid reader, bibliophile, lover of trees and animals, and a lifelong learner. She and her husband are pet parents to a sweet little Shih Tzu.

- Find out more, listen to Wing Academy Radio, and take the Vibrational Quiz at **www.DianeWing.com**.

- Check out her author website at **www.DianeWingAuthor.com**.

- Like her on Facebook **facebook.com/dianewingauthor/**

The Adventures of Autumn and Chrissy Begin Here

Only Chrissy, a cute little Shih Tzu, can unlock this mystery!

Autumn Clarke survived the car crash that killed her parents. To help her cope with PTSD, she adopts Chrissy, a Shih Tzu with a remarkable secret. Chrissy is also the only witness to the mysterious death of her pet parent. Autumn vows to find the truth behind his death with the help of Chrissy, the neighbors and an attractive detective. Can Autumn unravel the clues while trying to heal Chrissy's trauma and overcome her own devastating emotional wounds in the midst of a dangerous murder investigation?

"Chrissy the Shih Tzu may be the cutest sleuth on the job, but don't let that button nose fool you—it's perfectly able to sniff out a killer with a little help from her human friends. Great start to a fun new series!"

—Sheila Webster Boneham, Author of the award-winning *Animals in Focus Mysteries*

"Diane Wing does an excellent job of showing readers just how animals can communicate with us through images and actions when we are tuned into their frequency. Through the relationship between Autumn and Chrissy, Wing also shows the importance of therapy animals and how much they can help those who need them. Add in a sweet romance to the intrigue of the mystery and you've got a book that you won't want to put down."

—Melissa Alvarez, Intuitive, animal communicator and author of *Animal Frequency* and Llewellyn's *Little Book of Spirit Animals*

"Diane Wing has created a wonderfully endearing little character in Chrissy the Shih Tzu. It really shines through that the author is an animal and dog lover. I can see these books quickly becoming a cherished addition to the cozy mystery genre."

—J. New, author of *The Yellow Cottage Vintage Mysteries*

Learn more at www.DianeWingAuthor.com

From Modern History Press

CPSIA information can be obtained
at www.ICGtesting.com
Printed in the USA
JSHW010716250819
1185JS00007B/23